Nashville - Book Five - Amazed

Nashville - Book Five - Amazed

Inglath Cooper

Contents

Thomas Franklin has pretty much everything he's ever wanted in life.

Along with his two best friends in the world, he's part of Barefoot Outlook, a superstar band in the country music world. And if he's a little bit envious of the love Holden and CeCe have found in one another, he can accept the fact that he's had more than his share of good fortune.

Finding a girl like CeCe? Well, that's pretty much once in a lifetime.

In spite of Holden's constant harassment about his playboy reputation, Thomas is content to play the field. Until, that is, his past finds its way into the present when he agrees to do a charity gig in Virginia with Case Phillips. There, he crosses paths with the only girl who had ever stolen his heart for real.

The last thing Lila Bellamy expects on the night her best friend Macy takes her out for a birthday celebration is to find herself face to face with Thomas Franklin.

Seven years earlier, still haunted by the tragedy of her mother's death, Lila had found comfort in Thomas, and during the hours they were together, let herself forget for just a little while. It had taken nothing more than the light of day for her to realize that one night was all they were ever going to be.

Even though they had never seen each other again in all these years, Lila had never forgotten him. And not just because he had since become famous. Lila has another reason, one she's never wanted him to find out about. But as she well knows, life can change overnight. And Thomas Franklin is about to change hers all over again.

1

Thomas

Is This What I Was Waiting For?

The first time the phone rings, I ignore it.

I pull the pillow over my head and press it to my ear, trying to block the annoying screech of the Gomer Pyle *Shazam!* ringtone Holden put on my phone.

A hand reaches out to tap the side of my face. "Somebody's calling you, sugar."

I swat the manicured nails away and say nothing.

The phone begins to rattle again. *Shazam! Shazam!*

"Want me to turn it off?" I hear cigarettes in the voice, and at the same time, get a riff of stale alcohol.

"No, Sh—" I start to say her name, but realize I'm not sure I remember it. Sharla? Shauna? "I got it," I say instead, flipping over and grabbing the phone from the nightstand. Spotting Holden's number, I bark, "This better be good."

"Don't tell me you're still asleep?"

"It's the friggin' middle of the night. What else do you think I'd be doing?"

"It's twelve-thirty, shithead," comes his unperturbed reply. "As in the afternoon."

"What?"

"Since when can't you tell night from day?"

I open my eyes. The room is pitch dark. And then I see the small crack of light at the bottom of the heavy hotel room curtain. "Hell. I didn't mean to sleep this long."

"Where are you anyway?"

I try to think of the name of the town I picked off my GPS map last night when I decided I was too tired to keep driving, and can't for the life of me, recall it. "Somewhere between Nashville and Roanoke."

"That's helpful. Case needs to know what time you'll be getting in. He wants a little prep time before the show."

"Tell him I'll be there on time."

"Why don't you answer your dang phone and tell him yourself?"

I rub my hand across my eyes and stretch, bumping a long smooth leg that promptly tangles itself with mine.

"What bee got in your britches this morning. . .afternoon?" I correct quickly.

"The one that tells me you got drunk again last night, and there's a girl in your bed."

"Well, yeah."

Holden blows out a sigh. "When are you going to grow the hell up and quit acting like you need to prove you're not ever gonna settle down?"

"I'm not."

"What?"

"Settling down."

"CeCe thinks you're a jerk."

"Does not."

"Does too."

"She flat out adores me."

"That might be, but she's getting sick of giving the 'he's just not ready to be serious' speech to half the female population in Nashville."

"I didn't ask her to give that speech," I say, recognizing the defensive note in my voice. "And if anybody knows, you know I'm up front about my intentions, or lack thereof."

"You're fine with letting them all think you're a heartless di—"

"Hey, now. Play nice."

"No, that's my advice to you."

"Man, just because you and CeCe got it made over there in Love Shack Central, doesn't mean you get to dole out relationship advice to the rest of us losers."

"That what you call your nightly trysts? A relationship?"

"Did you just say trysts?"

"Hookups, whatever the hell you want to call them. There is such a thing as overuse, you know. You might just end up breaking it."

I laugh, unable to stop myself. "You're the one in danger of breaking it. I barely see you two except when we're on stage. Aren't you sick of each other yet?"

"No."

I can tell immediately his answer didn't come out with the lack of care he'd intended. Where CeCe is concerned, Holden can hide nothing. I've never seen anybody so flat out high on love as those two. And I'm not jealous. I'm not. Envious? A little.

But there's no way to resent what the two of them have found in each other. That would be like resenting the sun for its existence. It can't help that we have to have it to live. That's what it's like between those two. They need each other to actually survive.

And so I let the seriousness of his response go. Decide not to call him on it, even though he's giving me ten different kinds of grief.

"Seriously, man, give Case a call. For some reason, he's got it in his head you're not going to show."

"Course I'm going to show. Why would he think that?"

"I don't know. Maybe because you were half an hour late getting on stage in Lexington last week. Or it could be the rehearsals you keep missing." And then, more serious, "What's going on with you, Thomas?"

I feel my hackles rise, start to get defensive and then it fades away as quickly as it bloomed. "Nothing."

"That's not true. You haven't been acting like yourself for the past six months. Can I be honest?"

"By all means."

"I'm worried about you. Mind if I ask you why you agreed to go down there in the first place?"

I don't answer for a stretch of moments because the truth is I'm not too sure I know the answer myself. "You remember that gig we had in downtown Roanoke when we were juniors at Georgia?" I finally ask.

"Yeah," Holden says. "It was one of our first. We sucked."

"Pretty much," I agree.

"And you met that girl."

Part of me was hoping he wouldn't remember her, and another part of me is almost glad he opened the door. She's been at the edges of my thoughts pretty much the entire two weeks since Case asked me to join up with him in a fundraiser for families of victims of gun violence. "He wanted you and CeCe to be there, too," I say.

"We would have if CeCe hadn't already committed to that Hounds for Housedogs fundraiser. But I sure didn't think you'd want to go without us."

"Yeah, well, I guess anyway I can pay Case back a little bit for everything he's done for us, I'm glad to do it."

"Hold on. Is it my imagination, or did you just totally skirt the subject of the girl?"

"She was just a girl, Holden."

"Right. Don't forget I lived with you when she wouldn't return your calls and gave you your first taste of being on the other side of a one-night stand."

"Didn't you once call yourself my best friend?"

"Best friends tell each other the truth. And I think the truth was she yanked that ol' country boy heart of yours right out of your chest. That's why nobody else has ever gotten anywhere near it."

"Are you writing fiction now instead of lyrics?"

Holden barks a short laugh. "It wouldn't be called fiction. Maybe memoirs. If I remember right, she was a beauty."

"How would you remember? You were too drunk to walk straight, much less see straight."

"I wasn't that drunk."

"You sure you're not drinking right now? I know how alcohol likes to lead you down memory lane."

"No, I'm just wondering if you might have had something other than philanthropy in the back of your mind when you agreed to do this gig."

"That hurts, you know it?"

"What? It's not like I'd blame you if you gave her a call or something."

"She's probably married with five kids by now."

"Or she could still be single. Pining for you."

"Again, yeah right."

"Odds are she's seen your ugly mug in a magazine or two."

"I repeat, is this what best friends do for each other?"

"I'm just saying maybe you should call her."

"Did CeCe put you up to this?"

"No," Holden starts to defend automatically.

"She did, didn't she?"

Holden is quiet for a couple of seconds, and then, "I'll admit that she thinks you've gone a little overboard with the number of girls on your dance card."

"What's with you and the corny euphemisms?"

"You want it a little straighter than that? Here, you go. She thinks you pick women you're never going to fall in love with. She thinks you do it on purpose. And that it's got to feel a little bit empty."

"Most of the time, it feels pretty damn good." Even as I say the words, I hear my own lack of conviction.

"I'm not buying it. And neither is CeCe."

"I don't recall asking you to."

"All right, before you get all jacked up, answer this one thing. You like the image those rag tabloids are painting of you?"

"Honest answer? I couldn't care less."

"I know as well as you do," Holden says, "that they're not worth wasting an ounce of energy on. But you gotta admit, you do give them a lot of ammunition."

"Am I telling you how to live your life?"

"No," Holden says, and I hear in his voice that he's a little ashamed of himself.

"Look, Thomas, CeCe's concerned about you. And, well, I have been too, I guess."

"Y'all don't need to be worried about me. It's all good. Okay?"

"So good you could tell me the name of the girl next to you right now if I asked you?"

"As a matter of fact, I've gotta go. She's awake, and I've ignored her long enough."

I smack the end call button and toss the phone on the nightstand.

"If you were talking about me, that sure was sweet."

The girl whose name I still cannot remember slides her

hand up my chest and taps out a rhythm with her square-tipped nails.

"Especially since we've barely talked and all."

"We've talked," I say quickly, as if it's Holden who made the accusation.

She laughs a soft laugh. "I'm not sure those sounds we were making last night could actually be called words."

I run a palm across my in-need-of-a-shave face. "They could be a language in certain parts of the world."

She slides a little closer, slips her leg between mine. "We could say them again, if you like."

All of a sudden, I'm thinking about everything Holden just said. "I should hit the road."

"Awww," she says. "Can't you stay just a little longer?"

"I'd like to," I say. "But I have somewhere I really have to be." I sit up and all but vault off the bed, just as she reaches to grab my arm with a playful laugh.

"Surely, you've got ten minutes!"

"Afraid not this time."

She drops back onto the mattress, pouting against the pillow. "Will I see you again?"

I meet her hopeful gaze and make myself say the truth. "Probably not."

Her disappointment is immediately obvious. "I kinda knew you were gonna say that."

I start buttoning my shirt and find myself asking, "How?"

"Because you're one of those guys."

"One of which guys?"

"The kind who never lets his heart out to play with the rest of him," she says, still pouting.

"Is that how I strike you?"

"Yeah," she says. "It is. And I heard a little bit of what your friend was saying. So I know I'm right."

"Oh," I say. And then, "Look—"

"It's all right," she says. "No need to apologize. I'm a big girl. I figured you were too good to be true, anyway. You probably have like all kinds of skeletons in your closet."

"Oh, now I have a closet, huh?" I ask, teasing her.

She laughs, slides out of bed without bothering to take the sheet with her. "I'm going to take a shower. You decide you have that extra ten minutes, you know where you can find me."

She disappears in the bathroom then, the door clicking closed behind her. I let out a long whoosh of air and count to ten.

I get dressed, find my truck keys, wallet and phone, and then leave the room for the front desk to pay the bill. I'm out in the parking lot when I hear a screech coming from the middle of the hotel building. I look around, and the girl whose name I still cannot remember, if I ever knew it in the first place, is standing on the balcony of our room wrapped in a towel. She's waving her phone and screaming like she just won the lottery.

"I texted a picture of you to my friend, and she says you're Thomas Franklin! You are, aren't you?"

I shrug, no idea where to take this conversation from here.

"Ohhh, my word, I can't believe it!" She aims the phone at me and starts snapping pictures.

I shake my head, getting in the truck. I back up and then pull out of the parking lot. Through the rearview mirror, I can see her still snapping away.

Good. Gracious. Almighty.

♪

2

Lila

Got Your Back

I will be the first to admit that my job at Smart-Send is nothing to brag about. It requires the kind of mindless performance that leaves me enough energy at the end of the day to do the things I have to do when I leave here every afternoon.

For the past five years, I've worked a conveyor line in between two other women, Bertha Peters and Marsha Sowder, each of whom tip the scale at well over the two-hundred-pound mark and smell of antiperspirant that has fallen short of its declared abilities.

The highlight of their day is letting a box on the conveyor belt go before I'm ready for it so that my fingers get smashed between it and the one I'm finishing up. They consider this high entertainment.

This morning has been no different. They somehow got word that it's my birthday, and their objective has been to harass me beyond their normal acceptable standards. Bertha is sure I have a hot date lined up tonight where I'll be adorned with roses and fine jewelry.

"You takin' off early today?" she jeers, one hand propped on an ample hip. "Must take a while to get all that hair poofed and primped."

I continue placing the items in front of me in the cardboard box, choosing to ignore the taunt.

"Oh, she's not talking today," Marsha says. "She's probably picturing herself getting a diamond tonight, like that'll be her ticket outta here."

"At least that's a possibility for someone like her."

I turn to see Macy standing behind Marsha, looking like a mother bear that discovers somebody messing with one of her cubs.

Marsha turns around and gives Macy a laser look. "Anybody talkin' to you, Simpson?"

"If you're talking to Lila, that's the same as talking to me."

"And let me see if I've got this right. There's somethin' *you're* gonna do about it?"

Macy stares at her for a moment, then steps in closer so

that she stands virtually knee to knee with Marsha, who is literally double her size. Macy and I have been friends since elementary school when Terrence Moyer, who sat in the desk behind me during reading class, cut the end of my braid off. Macy cornered him in the hallway after class and gave him a bloody nose for his efforts.

Somewhere along the way, I became her personal project, which is, in a way, an honor because she's continued the crusade some twenty years running. As far as the rest of her life is concerned, she has an ADD-like attention span, getting bored with relationships before they ever actually define themselves.

"Why, yes," Macy says. "There is, actually. Later on this afternoon, when I've got Garth Meadows in that place where he *reeeally* doesn't want me to stop, I'm gonna take a little break and mention that I think he ought to fire your sorry butt and free up a spot on this line for someone who'll actually work instead of running her big fat mouth all the time."

Marsha's face turns red enough that the risk of stroke seems more than a likely possibility. She starts to say something, then appears to think better of it, turning back to the conveyor belt and the box she'd been working on.

Macy walks over to me, smiling big as if the last few

seconds never happened. "Happy birthday," she says, giving me a hug. "I've got a surprise for you."

I start to tell her that I don't need her riding to my rescue with Marsha and Bertha, but Macy is so full of cheer, I don't want to burst her bubble. "What is it?" I ask instead.

"After work," she says. "You'll see."

"Macy. . ." I begin to argue, hoping she doesn't have some kind of male stripper waiting in the parking lot at three-thirty. It wouldn't be the first time.

"Trust me, okay?"

I give her a look meant to remind her of the other times she's said this.

"Really. It's gonna be great."

We leave it at that, and Macy heads back to her workstation, while I wish for a believable excuse to leave early and avoid my mystery surprise.

The rest of the day unfolds as uneventful, Bertha and Martha both choosing not to test Macy's pull with Garth. When the factory bell rings at three-thirty, Macy is waiting out front for me.

"You ready for some fun?" she says.

"Don't you have some place to be?"

Macy wrinkles her forehead, and then says, "What? Oh, you mean Garth?"

"Yeah, Garth."

"I was just yanking their chain. Today, anyway," she adds, her grin mischievous."

"I've gotta pick up Lexie," I say.

"Yep. Then I'm coming over. And here's the surprise. My mama's gonna watch Lexie for you tonight, and we're going out."

"What?" I ask, disbelieving. "Macy. I can't do that."

"Why not? You know Mama will guard her with her life. And she's used to seeing her in Sunday school class."

"I know, but—"

"I know no one's the same as you, but you deserve this, Lila. And I'm not taking no for an answer."

The refusal rises up inside me. I can't even remember the last time I went out at night. But along with it, there is something else, the desire to go, to do something different. To shed responsibility, even just for a single evening. I feel guilty at the thought, but Macy pounces on my wavering like a cat on an unsuspecting mouse.

"She'll be fine. I promise. And it's your birthday, for heaven's sake. If anybody's earned a little celebrating, it's you."

"Are you sure your mom won't mind?"

"Are you kidding? You know she loves Lexie."

I feel myself caving. Maybe I do need a night out. "A couple of hours then. But I can't be too late, okay?"

Macy looks as if she wants to argue, but restrains herself. "We'll be there at six o'clock."

"All right," she says, climbing into the Land Cruiser and waving as Macy speeds away in her Mustang convertible.

♪

3

Thomas

Can't Blame the Fame

Case is waiting for me in front of the Hotel Roanoke when I pull up at just after five o'clock that afternoon. We'd talked a couple of times on my way down the Interstate, and I can tell by the look on his face, he hadn't actually been sure I was going to be here when I said I would be.

Each of the valet parking attendants standing nearby glances from Case to me and then back and forth again. Their expressions are just shy of neutral, when I suspect they want to run over and ask Case for his autograph.

To their credit, they refrain, and Case walks down the

steps and sticks his head inside the truck window on the passenger side.

"You made it," he says.

"Yeah. I meant to get here a little earlier, but—"

"You're good. You wanna run up and get a shower?"

"I'll be fast," I say.

"No problem. Long as we leave here by six."

I get out, and one of the valet guys runs up to take my keys and give me a ticket. We walk through the lobby, and Case waits while I get checked in. We take the elevator up to the second floor together.

"I appreciate your coming, Thomas," Case says. "Means a lot to me."

"No big deal," I say. "So what's the plan for tonight?"

"The show's at a venue over near Hollins College. The place is already sold out, so it should be a good night."

"Cool," I say.

"Gotta say I was kind of surprised you agreed to come," Case says.

I shrug. "We just finished up that last record, and getting out of town for a little bit sounded like a good thing. Plus you know I'm happy to do it for you."

"Thanks, man. By the way, I heard the roughs in the studio the other day. Y'all really knocked it out of the ballpark with this one."

"That means a lot coming from you. I think we all felt like we had something to say on this record."

"Do the world good to hear it," Case says. "When the audience tonight sees that you're the surprise special guest, I'm sure they're gonna feel like they got their money's worth."

"You'll make it more than that yourself," I say. "Your boys already set up?"

"Yeah, they've been over there since lunchtime."

We're quiet for a few moments, and then I say, "Haven't seen you in a while, Case. How you holdin' up?"

"Most of the time, okay," Case says, glancing down at his boots and shoving his hands in the pockets of his jeans. "You know, some days are harder than others."

I start to say I do know, but I don't really. The shooting had a different effect on every one of us, but it's Case who lost the most. And I've never wanted to act like I could even begin to understand what he feels. "You been down to visit Ms MacKenzie lately?" I ask, hoping he and CeCe's mother are still seeing each other. I imagine if anybody could help Case through this past year, it would be Ms. MacKenzie.

"Yeah," he says, "about every weekend."

I smile, glad to hear it. "She's a pretty special lady, no doubt."

"She is that," Case says. "How are you managing bachelorhood without Holden?"

"Managing," I say.

He shakes his head. "The two of them are playin' it pretty close to home these days, aren't they?"

"They're not sick of each other yet, that's for sure. They invite me over for dinner about every night. I guess they feel sorry for me."

"I don't think you're spending too much of your time alone now, are you, Thomas?" he asks with a knowing half-smile.

I don't bother to deny it.

"It can be a heady thing in the beginning," he says.

"What's that?" I ask, even though I'm pretty sure I know what he means.

"All the attention. The women. Mostly the women," he admits with a rueful grin.

I want to deny it, but I'm not going to fool Case Phillips, so I say, "Sometimes."

"Especially when you're lonely," he adds. He looks off, and his voice is a little distant when he says, "I sure didn't know what to do with it at first. Beck was a little guy, and his mama and I weren't getting along. She couldn't handle all the attention I was suddenly getting. I started spending more nights away from home with women whose faces I can't even remember now. When I think about the time I lost with my son because I made those choices, I—"

"Hey, Case. Don't do that to yourself. Beck adored you."

"I did some things as a father that weren't all that adorable."

"The state of being human," I say.

"That hindsight thing will bite you in the butt every time. And there's just something about youth that keeps us from realizing how every choice we make matters. What I would give if I could just go back and spend those nights with Beck when he was a little boy at home."

The regret in his voice is thick and emotion-filled. I can't think of a single word that would provide him with any comfort at all.

♪

4

Lila

What Love Is

The digital clock blinks a groggy two-thirty on the nose.

I lay on my thin mattress, staring at the bright red numbers on the digital alarm clock, fatigue so heavy on my chest that it feels as if there is no possible way I'll be able to pull myself up in three hours and start another day.

I glance at the monitor on the nightstand, straining to hear Lexie's steady breathing through the small speaker. As always, I feel relief for this proof that my daughter is fine, sleeping peacefully. Even through the fatigue, I feel a wave of gratitude, too, for this stretch of time that is mine and mine alone.

I open the drawer on the nightstand and pull out my

journal, scooting up and leaning back against the pillow with my hand on the leather cover. I smooth my thumb across the surface, its softness somehow soothing.

The book is one of the nicest things I own, a long-ago splurge that had taken a good-size chunk out of one of my paychecks and resulted in a two-week diet of Food Lion frozen green beans for me.

I open the cover and flip through the pages, the words blurring before my eyes. It's all there, the pain, the joy, the disappointment, and the elation of these past six years.

The book is nearly full now, only five blank pages left. I stare at the cream-colored emptiness, and the familiar need rises up inside me. I pull my pen from its holder along the spine of the book and set the tip to the paper.

The words flow up from some deep place, even though it's been a while since I've written anything. It's always been like this. The turning on of a tap, the rationing out of another small portion of the feelings inside me. When they come to life here on the page, it's only then that I manage to wrestle some sort of objectivity into the fears that sometimes get a chokehold on me.

When my pen finally goes still, I sit quiet for several minutes. And then I begin to write again, the verses coming in fragments, until the rough shape of a song begins to emerge. It feels easy tonight, maybe because I've arrived at another turning point, another birthday.

Twenty-five. It doesn't sound that old, really. Plenty of people my age are just getting started in the world, but inside, I feel a little ancient.

I open the drawer again and pull out my old tape recorder. It's the kind with the big rectangular buttons to push for play and record. It still works fine, and I pop in a blank tape, staring at the words I'd written until a melody begins to hum in my head. I test it out, keeping my voice low, glancing at the thin door that separates Lexie's room from mine.

I used to strum the tune with my guitar. It's been years though since I let myself play. A psychiatrist would probably have an interesting take on the why of it. But without the guitar, I can accept that the lyrics and melodies I continue to write will remain confined to the walls of this twelve by sixty-five trailer. To actually play them is to bring them to life, and I'd just as soon leave them dormant.

I sound out the tune, recording bits and pieces of it, until the chorus is complete. I work on the verses then, reaching for notes that tie back to it.

An hour later, the song is complete. I sing it through one time for the tape, then take it out of the player and label it with a black marker. I add the cassette to the shoebox collection beneath my bed, then put the journal and the tape recorder away.

The clock now reads five-fifteen. As much as I want to go back to sleep, it's time to get up. I throw my legs over the side of the bed, my feet protesting the wiry brown shag carpet that covers the trailer floor. Outside, I hear a dog bark. It's Brownie from one trailer back. Lexie and I call him Brownie, anyway. Rowdy Maxwell, Brownie's human, big as a small dump truck and as unenlightened as one of its spare tires, calls him Killer.

Brownie has been chained to the same tree for the four years Lexie and I have lived here. I've never once seen him loose and free to run or play.

Rowdy yells out a string of curse words now, that are intended to silence the dog.

Brownie's barking suddenly subsides with a yelp, and the dark outside the window goes silent again. Rowdy's training methods include the throwing of whatever happens to be closest to his porch side La-Z-Boy—hammers, empty beer cans, flower pots. I let myself imagine for a moment a fitting retribution for Rowdy, a stray lightning bolt that would permanently sear him to his polyester recliner, or perhaps a bullet through the back of his oily yellow **I Hunt** cap. Since I suspect God wouldn't endorse either one, I can only hope He has a better plan in mind for Rowdy.

I get up and head for the small bathroom, flicking on the light and glancing in the dingy mirror above the sink, my eyes widening at the reflection staring back at me. My hair hangs midway down my back, the ends in need of a trim. The blonde streaks that have been there since I was a child are its main redeeming factor, one of the few positive things I'd inherited from my mother. My eyes are blue, not a vivid, blinding blue, but dark, almost navy. The lashes that frame them are dark too, a contrast that makes people question the authenticity of my light hair.

Is it my imagination, or do I look different today?

Twenty-five. The number is a little shocking. Sometimes it doesn't seem possible that I'm not still a kid, trying to figure out how to get to the places I wanted to go in this life.

I lean in closer to the mirror and stare hard at my face. I think I look my age, except for my eyes. They look far older.

I push away from the sink and turn on the shower, pulling the plastic curtain away from the side of the tub and waiting a moment for the water to warm. I step in and turn my face up, letting the spray wash away my nagging fatigue.

I pick up the shampoo bottle and squeeze out the last bit, aware that it will be a week before I get paid and can buy more. The conditioner has been out for days, and the small bar of soap is one of the cheap motel soaps that Macy pilfers from the room where she meets Garth Meadows for their weekly get-together.

Garth is the foreman over at Smart-Send, the packaging company where Macy and I both work. I have no idea what she sees in the man. He isn't even passably good-looking. He just thinks he is, and maybe in the eyes of some women, that is as much as the same thing. To boot, he's married with three kids and a wife who would probably beat the dickens out of Macy if she ever found out Macy was fooling around with Garth.

Macy is like that, though. Which does nothing to explain why we're best friends. She's always loved a challenge, all the sneaking around and pretending there's nothing between her and the boss at work. I think for her, it's all that passes for high drama in a town where not much else does.

Macy grew up on soap operas, and she can recite the complete story lines for at least three. My theory is that the moment her fling with Garth is no longer a secret, that will be the moment she dumps him for good and moves on to a new installment.

I get out of the shower, towel dry, and then go back to the bedroom for a pair of jeans and a T-shirt. I don't bother drying my hair; I simply comb it out and pull it back in a ponytail.

In the kitchen, I put on a pot of coffee and pull a box

of oatmeal from the cabinet. I then head for Lexie's room where I flick on the small lamp next to her bed, standing for a moment, as I always do, to take in her sweetness while she still sleeps.

Lexie is a beautiful child. I can say this without fear of prejudice. I hear it all the time, from people on the street, in the grocery store, in the doctors' offices we visit with too-frequent regularity.

Here, still snuggled beneath her Barbie comforter, it's easy for me to imagine her as strong and healthy as any other little girl.

Her blonde hair is fine and silky, her skin like peaches at their most luminous, both pink and gold. Her hands are small and delicate, hands that look as if they might be gifted with a creative talent such as painting, or maybe she'll be musically inclined like me.

I sit down on the side of the bed, put my hand on her shoulder. "Lexie. Time to wake up, sweetie."

Lexie's eyes open and instantly find me; the light there is the payoff that keeps me struggling to get us from one day to the next. That light is our connection, proof of a bond of trust that doesn't need any words.

I put my hand to the side of Lexie's face and smile into her eyes. Lexie yawns widely. I slip my hands beneath the blanket and tickle her tummy. This is part of our morning ritual, and I need the fuel of my daughter's sweet giggles to get me going.

"Up and at 'em," I say, lifting her out of the bed and carrying her into the bathroom where I help her onto the toilet seat and wait for her to finish, before lifting her again and setting her on the special seat I had installed for the shower.

My back feels the strain, and I wonder how much longer I will be able to carry her like this. The thought brings with it a burn low in my stomach, the kind of looming problem I don't let myself dwell on. The truth is I don't know what I will do once I can no longer lift her, but then I hadn't known what I would do four years ago when a doctor told me she had cerebral palsy, that she would most likely never walk, never swim in the river I had grown up swimming in, and never ride a bike down country roads.

Most of Lexie's life has been a series of struggles to accomplish things that most people simply take for granted each day.

There are many things Lexie will never do. With God's grace, we have managed, trying not to look ahead for the next curve, but simply to keep negotiating the one we are currently in.

I turn on the faucet and let the water warm, testing it with my hand before turning the spray onto Lexie. Even at this early hour of the day, she loves the ritual, lifting her hands to try to catch the water as it sluices across her body.

Once we are done, I towel her dry and help her dress in a pair of flowery capri pants and a pink shirt. I then carry her to the wheelchair and fix her hair in matching braids.

In the kitchen, we both eat a quick bowl of cereal and drink a glass of orange juice. After that, we are out the door, and I use a small set of steps to help move Lexie to the back seat of my seen-far-better-days Land Cruiser. Once Lexie is inside, I stow the chair in the back.

"Need some help with that, Lila?"

I freeze at the sound of Rowdy's deep growl, not from fear, but something much more closely related to disgust. I close the back hatch and turn around with a clenched smile. "Got it. Thanks."

"That little girl sure is a lot of work for a tiny thing like you."

"Would you suggest I tie her to a tree?" The question is out before I can censor myself, my gaze cutting across the pitiful excuse for a yard to the bare spot where Brownie stands watching us, his tail wagging back and forth as if he still has hope that life can and will get better.

I try not to look at him because when I do I can hardly bear the thought that this is the only life he will ever know.

Rowdy walks over and leans against the Land Cruiser. He ducks a look at Lexie in the back seat, and I restrain myself from shoving him off the door. Even the thought of his eyes touching my daughter stirs me to a near rage.

"It works for my dog," he says, chuckling as if he's just delivered the funniest one-liner ever heard.

"Your dawg," I say, repeating his drawl, "is a prisoner."

"Well, how you figure, missy?" he says, getting a little irked now. "I let him loose, he'll just run off."

"You think?"

"I know."

"Gotta go," I say, starting the engine before I say something that gets me thrown out of the only roof we have over our heads.

He steps back, raises a hand. "Don't forget now. Rent's due on Monday."

As the resident landlord of the Sunflower Mobile Home Park, the name an oxymoron for the grim reality of the staggered rows of dated trailers, Rowdy takes pride in sparing no sympathy for late rent and has in fact personally escorted from the premises six families that I know of, piling their belongings in the back of his monster Chevy truck only to dump them just the other side of his property line.

I pull out of the rutted gravel driveway, feeling as if I need to go back and shower again.

Lexie's school is twenty minutes away, and we make the drive with her favorite songs playing on the Land Cruiser's old cassette player.

There is a funny rendition of "Happy Birthday," Lexie's favorite song on the tape. She claps her hands in offbeat rhythm, and I pretend for a moment that the song is for me, that Lexie knows today is my birthday.

As I wait at a stoplight in the center of town, the thought brings with it a poignant ache, one I try not to let myself feel too often. I'd long ago learned there's no point in living in the what-if. The only part of this life I have any control over is the now. And the truth is my daughter will never wish me happy birthday, will never grow up to live on her own, and will never call me to talk on the telephone.

And in all honesty, I don't know if this makes me sadder for me or for my daughter. My only comfort is that Lexie isn't aware of the magnitude of the loss.

That grief is mine alone.

♪

WE ARRIVE AT the Franklin School a few minutes later, a small yellow bus in front of us letting off a dozen or so children, each of whom has some visibly noticeable characteristic that makes them different from other children their age. I drive Lexie to school even though I could send her on this same bus.

I tried it once, thinking it would somehow help foster her independence, but something in the look on Lexie's small face as they pulled away made me feel as if I was deserting her. And so the next day, and every school day since, I've driven her instead.

Today, Lexie's classroom is already full, the other children who are like her in the restrictions they have to endure daily playing with an assortment of toys. Two little girls, one in a wheelchair, one standing with the help of a walker, smile big smiles when they spot Lexie rolling into the room.

I feel their welcome reaching out to my daughter even though no words are spoken. I've often wondered if the children are just happy to be in a place where they aren't different, where everyone else is mostly like them.

Their teacher, Mrs. Evans, walks up and says good morning to them both. She always has a sunshine smile for Lexie and the other children. To Mrs. Evans, the students here are special in the way of something to be treasured. Not in the way of something to be pitied.

That's the one thing I never want Lexie to be. And yet, I've seen it flit across the faces of people once they see past her prettiness and notice the wheelchair and all its implications. I can almost hear them thinking, *What a waste. She could have done so much with her life.*

That's the part that hurts beyond description. Because I

know they are right. Lexie could have. I would give my own life to make it so.

Mrs. Evans puts a hand on my shoulder and says, "I believe someone has a birthday today."

I meet her soft green gaze with a forced smile, appreciating the woman's thoughtfulness and yet at the same time reminded again that she remembered my birthday because she knows my daughter will not. She keeps a calendar of all the parents' birthdays so that each child can make something to give them.

"A birthday's always a good excuse to eat cake," I say.

"Clearly, you can afford to do so," Mrs. Evans says, giving me the kind of look my grandma used to give me when she thought I wasn't eating enough.

I lean down to give Lexie a kiss on the cheek. "Have a good day, sweetie," I say.

"We will," Mrs. Evans says, pushing Lexie to the center of the room.

At the door, I turn to look back, my heart contracting at the sight of my daughter surrounded by so much love. She belongs here, and it's clear that she is aware of this.

But as I leave the building, I am somehow more saddened by the thought than lifted up.

♪

5

Lila

One for the Road

With Lexie watching her favorite show on Noggin, I spend the better part of an hour in the trailer's stamp-size bathroom, taking a long soak of a bath with some salts I unearthed from the back of a cabinet. I wash my hair and paste on an intense conditioner I bought a couple of years before and never used. I file my nails to the short length I like them. After rinsing out the conditioner, I blow my hair dry, using a fat roller brush to straighten the slight wave of curl that settles in with the slightest onset of humidity.

I dress in the nicest jeans I own, a designer pair I discovered one day at TJMaxx with Macy. I suppose their reassignment to a discount store meant someone in Hollywood had deemed them no longer cool, but to me they're still worthy of special status. I pair a white scoop-neck T-shirt with them and then put on a little makeup, something I never bother with on a regular day.

Staring back at me from the dingy bathroom mirror is someone I rarely see anymore. I've grown used to the more-tired-than-tired reflection that greets me each morning and only manages to grow wearier by the time I brush my teeth at night. It feels nice to take time with the little things.

Once I finish getting ready, I scoop out some vanilla ice cream for Lexie to have while she watches one of the many *Barney* tapes I bought for her at the Goodwill store. No matter how many times she watches them, there is something about the big purple dinosaur that triggers happiness inside her with its own special light switch.

The phone jangles from its perch on the kitchen wall. I start to reach for it but decide to let the machine pick up the call.

I freeze at the sound of the voice.

"Lila. It's. . .it's your daddy." There is a long pause then, as if he is suddenly questioning his right to the title. "I know it's been a long time. It's your birthday. I hope you're having a good one." Another hesitation, and then, "I sure would love to see you sometime. And my grand—"

As if it has a mind of its own, my hand darts out to slap the delete button on the answering machine. Fury rises up inside me, and I can actually feel it turning my face a hot red. I draw in a deep breath and blow it back out again. With mechanical motions, I pick up the ice cream carton and place it back in the freezer.

How dare he?

These are the only three words I seem able to force through my mind, and they play over and over again, until I lean against the counter and blink them away.

All this time, and he picks today to call.

Why today?

I try to think how many years it has been, but a number won't stick in my head. A swirl of memories swim before me, pieces of the past that I long ago put in storage. My mama's face smiling down at me. . .the low growl of my daddy's truck as it pulls into our driveway every evening. . .the fights that were nearly certain to end the night.

I grab Lexie's bowl of ice cream and walk into the living room, sitting down beside her and holding it out like a peace offering.

She smiles her sweet smile, and I give her a bite.

A knock sounds at the door. "Come in," I call out, my voice shaking despite my best efforts to control it.

Macy walks through the door first, dressed in cowboy boots and jeans so tight it is a small miracle she managed to get them on. Mrs. Simpson, Macy's mother, is right behind her.

"How'd you know we weren't that awful landlord of yours?" Macy says, dropping her purse on the floor by the door.

"I'd have smelled him coming."

Macy laughs. "Oooh. Lila's sassy tonight, Mama. I think we're gonna have some fun."

"Now you girls have to behave," Mrs. Simpson says, her voice Southern soft, like the satin edges of a baby's blanket. "Just because it's Lila's birthday, you don't go out and forget your raisin'."

Grey hair pulled back in a bun, navy slacks and a white blouse, wire-framed glasses that tended to stay too low on her nose, Mrs. Simpson defines old-fashioned femininity. She can recite multiple books of the Bible — that is books, not verses — and actually makes as much effort to live what she believes as anyone I've ever known.

Macy, on the other hand, likes to test her mama's convictions on a regular basis. I've often wondered how Mrs. Simpson puts up with Macy's wild child lifestyle, but her patience is endless. She refuses to give up on getting her daughter back into church "one of these Sundays soon."

Mrs. Simpson steps forward and sits down on the couch next to Lexie, reaching in her oversize purse for a tissue and dabbing the white ice-cream mustache from Lexie's upper lip. "There you go, dear."

I kiss Lexie's forehead and stand up, certain that if I wait another moment to go, I won't be going at all.

Mrs. Simpson and Lexie are a picture of contentment as Macy and I walk out the trailer door a couple of minutes later. Macy leads me by the hand as if she knows I might bolt at any second.

She has no idea how right she is.

The guilt is by far the worst thing. There are times when I so much long for temporary freedom that it feels like acid eating a hole inside me. And then as soon as I get a little, the guilt sets in, and all I want to do is go home and hold my little girl until it goes away.

"Quit," Macy says, thwacking me on the arm as we slide into her yellow Volkswagen.

"What?" I say, clicking my seat belt.

"Thinking. Tonight is not about thinking. Tonight is about doing."

Macy backs up and pulls away from the trailer with a spit of gravel. I glance over at Rowdy's place, and there sits Brownie, chained up and watching us go, with the kind of longing on his face that needs no words for expression.

"And quit looking at that dog," Macy says, shifting gears so that we are breaking Rowdy's twenty-five mile-per-hour speed limit and then some. "Short of shooting that fat slob, Rowdy, there's nothing you can do to save him."

"That's what I love about you, Macy. Your endless stream of hope and optimism."

Macy reaches in the center console to pull out a pack of cigarettes, lights one and offers me the pack.

"No, thanks," I say. "I thought you quit those nasty things."

"I did. I'm quitting again tomorrow."

"Wouldn't it be a lot easier to quit for good?"

"Lets me practice my willpower."

"I'm sure one day I'll understand that."

Macy takes a deep pull and blows it out her partially lowered window. "You ready for your surprise?"

"How about we just catch a movie or something?" I say, wondering again if Macy has planned a night I will surely regret.

"A movie?" she says, looking at me as if I've just cast a curse on the whole plan. "Movies are for lame chicks who couldn't get picked up with a front-end loader."

"I like movies, and the last thing in the world I need is to be picked up."

"And when was the last time you experienced either one?"

I think for a moment. "Forrest Gump on DVD?"

"My point exactly."

I reach in my purse and pull out my cell phone, checking to make sure it has a signal. Macy snatches it from my hand and sticks it in her shirt pocket. "If it rings, I'll let you know. Otherwise, you'll will it into ringing, just so you'll have a reason to go home."

I roll my eyes and lean my head against the seat. "What's the point in celebrating another birthday anyway?"

"Well, the point is that we're still here, still kicking, capable of raising some serious hell."

"I'm capable of twelve hours worth of sleep, and that's about it."

"Oh, you've still got it, girl. We just gotta dig it up."

We take the 220 north ramp toward Roanoke. Macy cranks the music, and we drive the twenty minutes or so with Rascal Flatts as our soundtrack. I close my eyes and listen to the words, finally relaxing under their spell. I would be content with just this being my birthday surprise, riding in Macy's car with the wind blowing through the windows, the music making my pulse pound, nothing more than that expected of me.

In Roanoke, we head down 581 to the Peters Creek Road exit. A mile or so from Hollins College, Macy turns into a parking lot filled with cars. College kids stand in clusters, brown bags covering the bottles in their hands.

"Aren't we a little old for this place?" I ask. "And when are you going to tell me exactly what we're doing?"

"Now," she says. "We're seeing Case Phillips. He's doing a fundraiser here tonight. And he's got a special guest who hasn't been announced yet."

"Seriously?" I say, leaning back to give her a disbelieving look.

"Would I lie to you?"

"You've been known to," I say, smiling.

"Only when I thought it in your best interest," she says, defending herself.

"Macy, this is incredible. You shouldn't have done it. The tickets must have cost a fortune."

"Would you stop? Let me enjoy giving you your birthday present."

"Sorry. I didn't mean to sound ungrateful."

"We're here to have a good time. Let's get on it," she says, opening the car door and sliding out.

"How did you know about this?" I ask, getting out on my side.

"I keep my finger on the pulse," she says, smiling.

"I didn't know there was a pulse where we live."

We both laugh, and I realize it's been a long time since I laughed like this. I again feel instantly guilty for the thought, because while it's true, my life is as full of good moments as it is difficult ones.

We're parked next to a Saab convertible where a guy and girl are leaning against the hood, making out as if their curfew is imminent. The guy looks up at us with the slow-mo response of alcohol-numbed senses.

"Hey," he says, once he finally focuses, eyeing us both with interest. He steps back from the girl, and she makes an attempt to right the mini-dress that has made its way higher up her legs than even the designer must have intended. They both have the look of well-fed, well-groomed college students, and that air of confidence only found in people who have never had their status or their expected destination in life questioned.

"Hey," Macy shoots back, giving him a look and a smile that automatically raises the college girl's hackles. She puts a hand on the guy's arm, reestablishing her claim.

"You girls headed inside?" the guy asks.

"We are," Macy says, giving him a once-over that brings a new light of interest to his eyes. He steps away from the college girl as if he's been playing in the kiddy yard and just recognized an opportunity to move up to where the big boys play.

The girl glares at him and walks off. He shrugs and says to Macy, "See you in there?"

Macy grins. "You just might."

Halfway across the parking lot, I shake my head and say, "Was that nice?"

"Nothing wrong with a little teasing."

"Is he even legal?"

"He looks like he knows his way around the block."

"Like that means anything."

We reach the entrance where a line wraps around the side of the building. Macy takes one look at the chain of college students and walks directly up to the bouncer guy sitting on a stool at the door.

"Ladies," he says, "end of the line's back there."

Macy gives him a smile that could melt an icecap. "Evenin'. That sure is a long line."

"Yes, ma'am, it is. Gettin' longer by the second," he says, tipping his head toward the throng of guys piling out of an old green Cadillac.

"My friend and I are real anxious to see Case Phillips If we stand in that line, we might miss some of the performance."

"Good chance you will," he says, taking an ID from the next girl in line who barely looks old enough to drive. He gives it a cursory glance and then waves her in.

"I guess so with the careful scrutiny you're going to have to give all these IDs," Macy says. "I'm sure it's nearly impossible to tell a real one from a fake." She waggles her cell phone in the air. "Course I'd be happy to call up the local law enforcement and ask them to come on over and help you check their validity. We'd probably get in a lot faster."

Bouncer-guy looks at Macy through narrowed-eyes, clearly trying to decide if she is bluffing.

"Let me just check and see if they can help out." Macy starts punching numbers.

"All right, all right," he says, hitching his thumb toward the smoky interior behind him. "Devil only knows how many times you've pulled this one."

Macy kisses him on the cheek and saunters by. "Never failed yet."

He has the audacity to check out her behind, and as I follow her through the open door, meek as a church mouse, it occurs to me that it is always this way with Macy. She can take a guy to the mat, rob him of any last smidge of pride, and he actually ends up admiring her for it.

Macy grabs my hand and leads me through the throng of partying students, a few locals like us in the mix.

It's been years since I've been in a place like this, certainly not for Macy's lack of trying. It's hard, though, to go back to a place, or time for that matter, where I clearly don't belong anymore. It seems a far easier thing to keep my eyes focused forward.

Macy orders us each a beer from a lightning-fast

bartender — Corona with lime — pays for them, then hands me one. She clinks the side of her bottle against mine and says, "Cheers! And Happy birthday!"

"Thanks, Macy," I say and take a sip, the beer ice cold going down. "Have you checked my cell phone to make sure there aren't any messages?"

Macy pulls the phone from her pocket, taps the screen and says, "No calls."

"May I have it back, please?"

"Nope. Just as sure as I give it to you, you'll be calling my mama and findin' some excuse for us to get back home."

I roll my eyes and tell myself to be gracious. Macy has gone to some trouble to pull off this night.

She takes my hand and leads me over to a circle of guys who part like a wave beneath an oncoming cruise ship to allow us entrance. "Hey, fellas," she says, cranking the wattage on her smile.

There isn't one among them who has hit the twenty-one mile marker, and for Macy, it isn't an issue. For me, it would be too much like seducing the Sunday school class.

"How you girls doin'?"

I feel sure even Cesar Millan would declare this guy the leader of the pack. He isn't the tallest in the bunch, although at first glance, you'd think so. He holds himself the way a dominant dog does, body stretched tall and taut, the message clear, first to eat, first to pick from whatever female buffet happens his way.

Pack Leader gives Macy a once-over, approval glinting in his eyes, and then turns his attention to me. It only takes him a second to make his decision, and he is back at Macy, turning his veneered smile up to impossible-to-resist level. To his credit, Macy seems impressed, and the two of them step outside the circle to engage in a duel of wit.

"That didn't appear to hurt your feelings."

The man who utters this astute observation isn't part of the Sunday school class. Apparently, he's been watching from the sidelines.

He adds, "Frankly, I think he made the wrong choice."

"Well, thanks, but maybe you didn't hear my sigh of relief from where you were standing."

He laughs then, and I notice that he has a nice one. It is deep and resonant, if that's the right word. It echoes inside me, leaving something good behind.

I've always found a good laugh attractive, maybe because it's something a person can't fake. It either works, or it doesn't.

"Could I get you another beer?"

"Thanks, but I'm fine," I say, glancing over my shoulder.

"Waiting for someone?"

I direct my attention back to the guy in front of me. "No. No, I'm not."

"I'm David Graham by the way."

"Lila Bellamy."

"You from around here?" he asks.

"Half hour or so away."

"So what do you do when you're not hanging out listening to country music?"

Just the thought of trying to answer his question with any kind of accuracy weights me with exhaustion, so I shake my head and say, "Oh, you know, just normal stuff."

He leans back, gives me a long look. "Why do I get the feeling there's more to the story?"

Before I can answer, the thrum of noise in the club rises to another level, and then everyone starts to clap and cheer. I look toward the stage where band members are walking out to pick up their instruments.

"Do you know who the surprise guest is?" I ask.

"I do, as a matter of fact."

"Who?"

He smiles. "You'll see in a moment. I work for Case Phillips, actually. I'm his road manager."

"Oh," I say, feeling suddenly silly. "Wow. That's great."

The crowd starts to yell again, whistles and hoots. I

look at the stage where a tall guy in a baseball cap has just walked out and picked up a guitar.

I go completely still, as if I've been instantly frozen in place.

My heart kicks once, and then takes off at an erratic gallop. I feel sweat bead on my forehead. No way. It. Can. Not. Be.

"Thomas Franklin," David says close to my ear, "from Barefoot Outlook."

I try to respond, but for the life of me, I can't make a sound come out. I watch as he takes the stool in front of the mike while one of the players begins to strum a guitar. The crowd has gone completely silent, as if a mute button has been pushed. He starts out soft, the chords immediately grabbing me.

His voice follows, and the song spins its spell. I want to leave. I need to leave, but it's as if my feet are glued to the floor, and no matter what directives my brain tries to give, they aren't listening.

As soon as he hits the last note, the crowd goes wild with applause and cheering.

From the corner of my eye, I spot Macy walking toward the stage. I watch as she walks straight over to Thomas. And then I realize what this whole night has been about. She wouldn't. She wouldn't!

I open my mouth to call her name, but no sound comes out.

They chat for a few moments, and then I see the look of surprised disbelief cross his face. Macy points my way, and his gaze spotlights where I'm standing until he finds me. His eyes widen, and then a slow smile breaks across his face. He taps the microphone to get the crowd's attention and says, "I've just been told there's a special birthday girl in the house tonight. Lila, this one's for you."

He sings a solo rendition of the song I've heard every year of my life in one version or another, none of which ever affected me like this. His voice caresses each word, and by the time he's sung the last words — "happy birthday to you" — I feel as if I've just received a deep-tissue massage, and it is all I can do to keep my legs from buckling.

There is a pause then as the last notes fade away, and he says into the microphone, "Lila Bellamy. Could you come up front, please?"

Too stunned to move, I stand perfectly still. David leans back and gives me a questioning look before saying, "Go on. He won't bite."

At the side of the stage, Macy starts clapping and then others start to join in. Before long, the whole place comes alive with it, and what else can I do except start walking?

I use the time it takes me to weave my way through the crowd plotting various ways to pay Macy back for this act of kindness. As I walk past her, fully intent on ignoring her, Macy takes my arm and forces me to look at her, her face and voice uncharacteristically serious. "Go for it, okay?"

She then puts her hands on my back and pushes me forward. Suddenly, I'm on the stage with Thomas Franklin beckoning me over.

My feet have become concrete blocks, and it's all I can do to force myself to pick them up and walk the short distance to where he's waiting. My mind races with possible scenarios of what will happen once I get there. A sweet peck on the cheek. A serenade, maybe. Macy is nothing if not imaginative, and persuasive too.

But what actually happens, all but knocks the wind from my chest.

"Hey, Lila," Thomas says in his buttery, sandpaper voice, his eyes capturing mine. "I hear you know how to sing a song."

I stare at him as if he has just released a string of Greek words I've never heard before. "I—no, not really."

He hands me a guitar a band member has just passed him. He then offers me the stool. "Happy birthday," he says away from the microphone. "Although I feel like I'm the one getting the present."

If it is possible for fear to actually freeze the blood in a person's veins, then that's exactly what happens to me. Terrified, I can barely grasp the neck of the guitar because my fingers are shaking so badly.

While I want to be furious with Macy, tell Thomas this is a crazy mistake, that I had no idea she was going to do this, I can't even begin to find the words.

"The stage is yours," he says. "Let's hear what you've got."

Something in his tone connects with my terror and yanks the plug on it. It drains from me like water from a tub, and I realize people are staring at me, waiting to see what I'm going to do.

It hits me then that this is probably the last time I will ever have the opportunity to sing in front of anyone other than the reflection staring back at me from the bathroom mirror.

I feel the tug of long-ago dreams, and I sit down on the stool, positioning the guitar on my knee. It is a very nice one, a little big for me, but really nice. I test a few chords and instantly recognize the guitar's superiority to anything I've ever played.

I strum a beginning, leaning in to the mike and saying, "This song is called "Amazed." It's about how I want to live my life without ever becoming jaded about the things that really matter."

My voice cracks, and I tell myself I can't do it. It's been years since I sang in any kind of public setting. This is insane.

Silence hangs in the room, and I catch Macy's gaze, trained on me with such conviction. She believes in me, in the way that only the truest of friends can, and with that as my guidepost, I take a deep breath, and start over. This time my voice lifts and carries each word of the song to its intended place.

The room goes completely silent except for the tinkle of glass from the bar area. I remember then what it feels like to captivate an audience, show them a small piece of me, watch as understanding lights their faces. Just as I let the song fade with a few emotional notes, I feel the relief I always felt years ago when I realized I had made that connect.

The crowd begins to clap, the noise rising to the rafters of the room. Several voices call out for more, and others join in. I glance out from the stage where Thomas stands next to Macy.

He walks over, dips his head to my ear and says, "Damn, girl. I had no idea."

"Why would you?" I say, keeping my voice light. "We didn't exactly concentrate on conversation that night, did we?"

I feel him flinch a little, and then he says, "Will you wait for me after the show?"

"I can't stay," I say quickly, suddenly certain of that fact if nothing else. "And if you don't get back behind the mike, this crowd is going to stage a riot."

I finally let myself fully look at him, and only then realize I've been avoiding it. He has the kind of good looks that don't really seem fair when he's also been blessed with such an incredible voice. But they go together, that's for sure.

I stand up from the stool and force myself to meet his gaze. "Thank you, Thomas. That was the best birthday present I've ever had."

The band starts up, and I hand the microphone to him. "It was nice seeing you again."

"Lila, wait," he starts, but I'm already leaving the stage and making my way through the crowd to where Macy is standing. The look on her face tells me she has no idea whether I am going to hug her or slug her.

"One day you'll thank me?" she says with a questioning smile.

"Did you know he was going to be here?"

"Maybe?"

I sigh, shaking my head, even as I try to understand that her intentions where I'm concerned are always good.

"I know you think you were doing a good thing for me, but Macy, you know what I have to lose."

"Do I? The way I see it, there's only room for you to gain a little."

"I don't want anything from him. I never have."

"That's not the point."

My cell phone rings from its place in Macy's shirt pocket. She snatches it out and turns her back to answer it.

"If that's your mama, give me the phone," I say, trying to reach for it.

Macy dodges my effort, but then goes suddenly serious. I watch her face fall and feel the contents of my entire being drop to the floor.

"What is it?" I ask, barely able to suppress the panic in my voice.

"We'll be right there, okay?" Macy says and snaps the phone closed.

She looks at me then, putting a hand on my shoulder as if she might need to steady me. "It's Lexie. She's had a little bit of a seizure. Mama's at the hospital with her now."

Panic floods through me. "What? Oh, no! We have to go. We have to go!"

Macy takes my hand and starts leading me through the crowd. She plows through the bar, like a swimmer caught in a riptide, determined to break the current. The exit seems as if it's miles away. And all I can think is that I never should have come to this place tonight.

I don't belong here.

I should have been home with my daughter.

That is the only place where I belong.

♪

6

Thomas

You Just Never Know

It's all I can do to get through my set. There are a few times when I actually think I'm not going to be able to remember the words to the next verse in front of me. All I can think about is following Lila.

But I keep my feet planted firmly on the stage. I promised Case, and I can't go back on my word to him. So I force myself to tune out everything except the forty-five minutes in front of me.

When the end of the set finally comes, I thank the crowd for their attention and walk off stage to where Case is waiting just out of sight, guitar strapped across his shoulder.

"So, who is she?" he asks me with a half-smile.

I make an attempt to shrug as if it's all casual. "Someone I met several years ago when Holden and I were playing here in Roanoke."

"I take it she made an impression on you."

"Never saw her again as a matter of fact, until tonight."

"She's got quite a voice."

"Yeah, that was a surprise to me."

"Planning on seeing her tonight?"

"I don't really think she's interested in seeing me."

Case pulls back and gives me a long look. "Well, that certainly sets her apart from the crowd. All the more reason you better go after her," he says, with the first real smile I've seen on his face in a long time. "Must be something special about her. Hey, thanks for the performance," he adds. "You were awesome out there."

"A little distracted, I'm afraid," I admit.

"Then nobody realized it but you. I'm on. See ya' later."

Case walks out and the place erupts in a roar of applause. I grab my things and head outside to the truck. I had parked in the back of the building where Case and the band bus parked. Thankfully, no one is around as I hit the remote and unlock the door. I slide inside and sit for a minute with my arms draped across the steering wheel, trying to absorb everything that happened in there tonight.

Gut instinct tells me I should just drive back to the hotel, head up to bed, and order some room service. But I keep picturing her face and hearing her voice on the notes of that song, and I really want to see her again. The likelihood of the two of us running into each other tonight has to be somewhere in the same statistical range as this small Virginia city getting hit by a meteor.

So how had it happened?

My guess is her friend had something to do with it. I know without a doubt that Lila had no idea I would be here. Or she wouldn't have agreed to come.

To this day, I have no idea why she took such an aversion to me. After the fact, anyway.

I left her that morning almost seven years ago, fully expecting that we would see each other again. I *wanted* to see her again. But when she refused to answer my phone calls or return my emails, I eventually chalked it up to her deciding I had been a very bad idea.

And at the time, I probably was.

Considering all of that, I'm pretty sure I should leave her alone now. There's not an ounce of logic to me pursuing her an inch farther. Even so, I know I'm going to.

So how do you find somebody who doesn't want you to find them?

I pick up my phone and tap the screen.

Google. Of course.

♪

I FIND THE ADDRESS in the White Page Directory, tap the information into my GPS, surprised to see that it's some forty-five minutes away.

I'm pretty sure that this could be a really bad idea. Who's to say there's not a husband waiting for her at home? Maybe she and her friend were simply having a girl's night out.

I can't picture that scenario, but maybe that's more because I'm hoping it isn't true. When in all reality, it could be.

I crank the radio and drive with the window down, letting the music and the cool night air blow away all my reservations as to why this is a really bad idea.

I'm there before I'm ready to be. The GPS on my phone indicates a left-hand turn just ahead. I hit my blinker and brake at the same time, spotting a sign painted on an old board that reads: "Rowdy Pike's Sunflower Mobile Home Park. Enter at Your Own Risk."

I'm wondering if the GPS has steered me wrong, but the address is 150 Pike Road, so I guess it's right. I let the truck roll slowly down the gravel road, first one tire, then another dropping into pothole after pothole.

A quarter mile or so down, I see two long rows of trailers, one on my left, one on my right. Each is marked with a painted number on the top corner.

I turn into the small parking spot for the one marked 150, the lights of the truck sweeping across the rusted exterior of the seen-far-better-days mobile home.

There's no other car here, and all the lights are off. I should leave. No doubt about it. I should leave.

But I open the door and slide out, something I can't even explain pulling me to the front of the trailer where I knock softly and say her name, "Lila?"

There's no answer, and I step off the small porch just as I hear a door hinge creak open.

A voice calls out, "You got a reason to be hangin' around here in the dark?"

The question is a little slurred and a lot accusing. "I'm looking for Lila Bellamy."

"Well, I reckon you can see she ain't here."

A dog whines from somewhere behind him. In the dark, I can just make out the silhouette of a dog chained to a barrel that appears to be doing an impersonation of a dog house.

"You know when she'll be back?" I ask.

"I ain't her secretary."

The dog whines again, and the man snarls over his shoulder, "Shut up, you stupid mutt."

Anger unfurls inside me, and my fists clench automatically. "Do you expect that she'll be back tonight?" I ask, keeping my tone deliberately even.

"My guess would be no, since the rescue squad came in here earlier and took that kid of hers to the hospital again."

"Kid?" I ask, realizing the word sounds as stunned as I feel.

"Always something wrong with her."

"What do you mean?"

The man shrugs, his impatience level obviously rising. "I don't know. She's crippled up or something."

"Would you happen to have any idea which hospital they took her to?" I force the words out in as neutral a tone as I can manage, when what I'd like to do is relocate his nose for him.

"No, I wouldn't happen to have any idea which hospital they took her to," he mocks back. "Unless you got some reason to be here, this is private property, so you'd best be going."

The dog whimpers again. This time, he throws the beer can he's holding in the direction of the barrel-doghouse. It pings off the side, making a bullet sound that sends the dog flying inside the center of the barrel.

I have never wanted to hit someone so badly in all my life.

I ball my fists into a knot and walk back to the truck, putting one foot in front of the other until I'm safely inside and backing out of the driveway.

I allow myself the pleasure of envisioning a few possible responses to dealing with that scumbag, all involving actions that would most likely land me in jail most of the rest of my life.

I take the pothole-strewn driveway at a speed that spits a stream of gravel behind me. I can only hope one hits him in the head.

I'm back on the main road, trying to figure out where to go from here when my phone rings. Holden's name appears on the screen at the same time Gomer Pyle declares Shazam! I answer without letting myself consider all the reasons I don't need to be talking to him right now.

"How'd it go?" Holden asks right off.

"It was a good show," I say, keeping my voice neutral.

"You back at the hotel?"

"Not exactly."

"Another town? Another girl?"

"Not exactly."

"You sound weird."

"It's been a weird night," I admit.

"What? You run into Lila?" He asks the question in a joking voice, as if it's the very last thing he expects me to say yes to.

"Actually, yeah, I did."

"What?"

"Yeah, for real," I say.

"How the heck did that happen?"

"It's her birthday. A friend of hers brought her to the show. She asked me if Lila could sing a song."

"Lila sings?"

"Yeah," I say. "Pretty great, actually."

"Are you with her now?"

"No. Just looking for her."

"All right, you lost me somewhere between Lila sings and looking for her."

"She left the show before I was done, and I decided I'd look her up."

"And?"

"And some IQ-challenged redneck just told me she has a daughter who got taken to the hospital tonight for something."

"She has a daughter?" Holden sounds as shocked as I'd felt.

"Apparently."

"Is she married?"

"Rowdy the Redneck didn't mention it. I guess she could be."

"How old is the girl?"

"I don't have any idea."

"Maybe you oughta find out."

"Why?" It occurs to me then what he's implying. "Are you crazy? I was with her one night, Holden. After which, she gave me the boot."

"Last I heard, it only takes one night. Boot or not."

"That's insane," I say.

"If you're that sure, then I recommend you point the truck toward Nashville and floor it."

"I am sure," I say.

"Okay. So we'll see you back here tomorrow?"

"CeCe wants to know if you can come over for dinner tomorrow night. Heads up, there's someone she wants you to meet."

"You know, maybe I just need to swear off women for a while."

"You could do that," Holden says. "But you won't. CeCe thinks you'll like this girl."

"I thought she was busy warning every female she meets that I'm bad news."

"Hey, are you asking me to explain the way girls think?"

"No, because I don't think you have any more idea than I do."

"You're right about that. So we'll see you here tomorrow night then?"

"Later," I say, hanging up without giving him a definite answer either way.

A convenience store sits up ahead, and I pull into the parking lot so I can think for a minute. I don't have a single doubt in my mind that the smart thing for me to do is exactly what I just implied to Holden I would do. Head on back to Nashville.

I lean back and stare up at the night sky through the sunroof, my thoughts at war. I keep seeing her face as she sang that song tonight. And I can't quit thinking how right she had looked there. How happy it had obviously made her. But then seeing where she's living, next to that sorry excuse for a human being. And finding out that her daughter has some kind of problem.

The jerk's words come back to me then. "I don't know. Crippled up or somethin'."

Why would she be living in a place like that? Clearly, she could use some help. Whether she'll let me or not, I have no idea. But all of a sudden, I'm absolutely sure that I want to offer. And not because I think for a second that the child could be mine. She would have told me. I don't see her keeping something like that from me. Probably some guy who refused to take responsibility, leaving her to do the best she could.

I pick up my phone and do a local search for the nearest hospital, give the GPS the address and then pull back onto the road. I'm just going to let her know I'd like to help out. Find out where I can send her some money. Then be on my way back to Nashville.

And eventually, it will seem like this night never happened. Just like the only other night I ever spent with her.

♪

7

Lila

Just One Song

She looks like an angel.

I've thought this so many times. Sitting by the hospital bed, running my hand through my daughter's silky blonde hair while she sleeps, I wonder how I could ever think I needed anything more than this child in my life. Just the thought of losing her makes me feel as if my chest has been opened with a kitchen knife and my heart removed with bare hands.

This isn't the first time we've been here, or the first seizure Lexie has ever had. I never handled one any better than the other. They terrify me and leave me as emotionally exhausted as they leave Lexie physically spent.

I glance up and find Macy and her mother watching us from the doorway. Mrs. Simpson had done all the right things, called 911 immediately, but I can see that she's shaken.

I know the feeling of realizing that you are the only person standing between my beautiful little girl and possible death. I feel guilty for putting that responsibility on Macy's mother.

Macy steps around her mom and comes into the room. She stops at the bed and watches Lexie for a moment, taking in the even rise and fall of her breathing. "Thank God," she says.

"I know." My voice breaks under the words, and Macy squeezes my shoulder in understanding.

"Promise me something?"

"What?" I ask, glancing up at her.

"That you're not going to let this be a sign that you can't ever go out again and do something for yourself."

"I won't," I say, completely unconvincing even to my own ears.

"You will, too."

I don't bother to deny it this time. I don't believe in signs, but I do believe in reminders. This is that for me. A reminder of where I am supposed to be.

Macy sits on the corner of the bed, places a hand on Lexie's thin leg beneath the blue hospital bedspread. "You were incredible tonight, you know," she says.

I shake my head. "Some things aren't meant to be revisited. I never should have done that."

"You can't take this to mean that," she says, exasperation in her voice. "Sometimes, Lila Bellamy, I think I need to get out one of my good dresses and throw you a big ol' pity party!"

If I wasn't so tired and guilt-riddled, I might have actually smiled, except it's clear Macy isn't trying to be funny. "I'm not asking for pity, Mace."

"No. You don't ask for anything. Good heavens, girl, you had those people eating out of your hand with one song. Just one song! That's a gift, Lila. And you've thrown it all away. It might as well not even exist."

"I did no such thing. It didn't go anywhere. But my life isn't just about me. I thought you understood that."

"Of course, I do. I love this little girl nearly as much as you do. But I also love you. And what I don't understand is why you think you have to give up all your dreams just because you got pregnant and had a child. Is it really fair that Thomas has gone on with his life when you haven't?"

"We were one night. And I've gone on with my life in exactly the way I wanted to. Lexie is everything to me."

Macy is quiet for a bit, and I can tell she's weighing what to say next.

"Do you really think it's right that you've kept her from him?"

I pull back and give her a long look. "Are you questioning what I've done just because Thomas is playing in Roanoke for one night? He's passing through. That's the life he leads."

"I'm questioning it because you're barely able to make ends meet! It's too much for one person, Lila. Too much for you."

"Stop. Macy, stop," I say, pushing back my chair and standing. "I don't want her to hear this."

"She's asleep, Lila. And you need to hear it."

"Hey."

We both turn to the doorway at the same time. Thomas is now standing there next to Mrs. Simpson, hands shoved in his pockets, a look of complete uncertainty on his face.

"What are you doing here?" I ask, panic welling up inside me so fast that I feel instantly sick.

"I'm not really sure," he says, his voice low and honest.

Macy walks to the door, reaches for his hand and pulls him inside the room. "Come in, Thomas. Mama and I were just leaving. Lila, I'll touch base with you later."

With that, she leads her mom down the hall and to the elevator.

The air in the room has become electrified. My heart is beating so fast I can feel it in my throat. I want to pause everything and rewind to earlier in the day when I could have refused to go out with Macy. When I could have stayed home with Lexie, and none of this would have happened.

I watch as he turns his head to look at Lexie where she is still asleep in the hospital bed. He stares at her and then walks over to stand beside her, looking down at her sweet face for a long time.

I see the recognition as it dawns on him. His lips part slightly, and he sucks in a short whoosh of air as if someone has just slammed a fist into his midsection.

It will do no good for me to deny what he is thinking. He is there in her features. I am there in her features. The blend of the two of us is unmistakable.

When he does turn to face me, he suddenly reaches for my elbow and propels me out of the room. I feel the anger in him, tight and coiled. He walks me to the end of the hall where a small waiting room for families of patients is currently empty. He closes the door behind us and locks it.

I force myself to walk to the opposite corner, staring out the window at the cars four floors below us, my arms wrapped around my waist as if I can hold all my fear inside.

"How could you do this?" he finally asks, each word forced from him through gritted teeth.

"Thomas—"

"How could you not tell me?"

I try to draw in a deep breath, but the air feels trapped in my chest. "Because I didn't need your help."

"My help? I'm fifty percent of what it took to make that little girl. My help? I had a right to know, damn it!"

"One night doesn't give you the right—"

He slams his fist through the air, connecting with the palm of his other hand. "Yes, it does give me the right! It took two of us to make her."

"And one of us to mess her up? Are you going to add that?"

"What? No. I—"

I start to cry then, sobs rising from inside me so quickly that I cannot hold them back.

"What do you mean, Lila? She's beautiful. She's perfect." And then in a panicky voice, "What's wrong with her? Is she going to be all right?"

I press my fist to my lips and will myself to stop crying. When I finally answer him, my voice is so low that he leans in closer to hear me. "She has cerebral palsy, Thomas."

"What?" Shock reverberates through the question.

"I didn't know until just after she turned three."

"What is it? I mean I've heard of it, but—"

I cross my arms tight around myself and try to find the words. "It's caused by a brain injury. Most likely before she was born. While her brain was still developing."

He says nothing for a long time, as if he's processing every word of what I've just said. "And you never thought you might need my help?" he says, the words low and uneven.

"I didn't want you to feel obligated—"

"But wasn't I?"

It's not what I expected him to say. And so I don't know how to answer. Finally, I manage, "I won't say that night was a mistake, Thomas. I would give my life for my daughter, but we both know it was never something that was meant to last. I didn't want to be a girl who trapped you into—"

"Damn it, Lila! That was an awfully big decision for you to make for me."

"I had to do what I thought would be best for Lexie and for me."

"And you couldn't even give me the opportunity to do the right thing?"

I meet his gaze then, and the hurt there is not what I expected to see. "Thomas. Do you think you would be where you are now if I had told you? You would never have gone after your dream. And I would be the one who kept you from doing it."

"That's not fair," he says.

"Maybe not. But I do believe it's true."

He stares at me for a long, uncomfortable string of moments, his jaw set and hard. "You have no way of knowing that."

I can see that I've hurt him, and that was never my intention. Had I been wrong to shut him out? Suddenly, I don't know, and a tidal wave of confusion washes over me, taking with it any ability I have to find logic in this.

But before I can say another word, Thomas yanks open the door and walks out, his boots making a hollow, echoing sound on the hospital's spotless tile floor.

♪

8

Thomas

What You Can't Get Back

I've never wanted to hit something so much in my whole life.

My fists itch with the need, and I keep them balled up until I reach the truck in the hospital parking lot. I yank open the door and slide inside, gunning the engine as soon as I hear it crank.

The truck fishtails onto the street, and I floor it through the first stoplight. But then common sense crashes over me, and I hit the brake hard, slowing down to meet the speed limit.

I don't know what to think first.

I have a daughter.

A little girl.

A beautiful little girl.

Her name is Lexie.

She's been alive for six years, and I knew nothing about her.

How can that possibly be?

I think about the look on Lila's face when she'd seen me standing in the doorway. The instant terror in her eyes. Could she really think I might try to take Lexie away from her? Or that I would reject them both?

My heart and brain balk at this, but then how would she have known any different? Other than the fact that the chemistry between us had been instant and electric, we knew little else about each other. We hadn't even been together for twelve hours.

And yet those hours had been completely life-changing. Life-creating.

I flick on the radio in an effort to slow my thoughts long enough for me to process them.

CeCe's voice flows into the truck on the words of our latest single. My voice comes in behind hers, and I reach over to turn it off, not needing the reminder of why Lila might have thought I wasn't ready to be a father.

I'm halfway back to Roanoke when I pull into a McDonald's parking lot. I find an out-of-the-way spot and cut the engine, dropping my head onto the back of the seat and staring up at the sky.

I pick up my phone to call Holden, but just as quickly decide I'm not ready for that. I need to know what I think about this first, take the pieces apart and look at them one by one until I can absorb the complete truth.

For whatever reason, Lila hadn't trusted me with the fact that she was pregnant. No matter how I try to process this, the realization has painfully sharp edges.

Had she gone through it all alone? I remember that she told me her mother had died. That she was an only child. I can't remember if she said anything about her father.

All the anger that propelled me out of the hospital less than half an hour ago suddenly slides away, like mud down a rain-pummeled hillside. In its place, I just feel an incredible sadness. Like a loss. Grief for something I know I will never get back.

The birth of my daughter. The first six years of her life. And the opportunity to be a part of doing whatever could possibly be done to help her.

I don't want to judge Lila for the decisions she made. None of it can be redone, and if I'm not sure of anything else, I'm sure of her love for Lexie.

Maybe she was right to shut me out back then. I'll never know the answer to that. But I'm not going to be shut out again. I want to know my daughter. I want her to know I want her.

♪

I WATCH HER FROM the doorway for a few seconds, wishing I could somehow freeze-frame this picture.

Lila is leaning over the bed with her cheek on Lexie's hand. Her eyes are closed, and I'm not sure if she's asleep or just resting.

"Lila," I say eventually, keeping my voice low so that I don't wake up Lexie.

She sits up with a start, stands and puts a hand to her chest. "Thomas. I didn't know you were there."

"Can we talk for a minute? This time I promise to be rational."

She looks as if she wants to say no, but nods once and waves me out of the room. We go back to the waiting area, and it's still empty.

"Thomas," she says with regret in her voice. "I know I haven't been fair to you. I never meant to-"

"Don't," I say.

She looks at me, uncertainty clouding her eyes. I walk closer and reach out to her. She resists me at first, holding herself so stiff that I wonder if she might break if I force her to yield. But the truth is I need to comfort her as much as she needs me to do it. So I reel her in slowly, but with determination, until she folds herself into my arms, burying her face against my chest where my shirt muffles the sound of her crying.

I don't know how long we stand there, but I feel myself absorbing every ounce of the pain I feel inside her. Several minutes pass before I can bring myself to ask the question I have to ask. "I know it was just one night, but did I really seem like the kind of guy who wouldn't have done the right thing?"

Even before she says a word, I think I know the answer. I know who I was then. And how I must have looked to her. At the very beginning of chasing a dream I had every intention of catching. I remember some of the things I said to her that night. And from here, I guess I can understand what she would have thought. That even if I did agree to be a part of Lexie's life, I might eventually come to resent it for the things it kept me from doing.

I can see this, and I want to flat out deny it, but I don't know if I can. Because right now, I'm at the top of the mountain. The view from here can in no way be compared to the view from where I stood then.

I'd like to think I would have said the right thing, done the right thing. But I don't know if I would have or not.

"I'm sorry," I say, rubbing her back in an effort at comfort. "I shouldn't have said those things I said earlier.

I can see how much you love her. You've devoted your life to her, and I—"

"—wasn't given the chance," she finishes for me. She pulls back, wipes a hand across her face and says, "I should have given you that chance. But I—" She stops, glances off, and then, drawing in a deep breath, says, "I wanted to believe that you would want to know, but I guess it's been my experience that most of the time, people just end up disappointing you."

We stand there, quiet, for a long while. I want to argue with her. But I hear the conviction in her words. Have no idea what she's basing them on. I just know she believes they're true. And it feels good to hold her like this. I don't want to pull away. I don't want her to pull away.

"How about we start from here," I say, "and you give me a chance to be a stand-up guy? I promise you I'll do my best to live up to it."

She looks up at me then, and I see the fear in her eyes. "You can't take her from me, Thomas. She's all I have."

"Lila," I say, hearing my voice break across her name. "I would never. . ." I stop and then say, "Let's just start from here. We'll figure out how as we go."

♪

9

Lila

A Rowdy Retribution

The doctors release Lexie at just after seven the next morning. Thomas left the hospital at four to drive back to Roanoke to shower and change clothes, promising to be back within a few hours.

I should call him and ask for a ride home, but I can't bring myself to do it. I'm use to taking care of us myself, and the thought of leaning on him at all will take some getting used to.

I call the town cab instead. Harmon Quinn is thrilled to have a passenger before noon, and we head out of town with Lexie's wheelchair sticking out of the trunk.

"It sure is worrisome when these young'uns get sick, ain't it?" Harmon says now, glancing in the rearview mirror at Lexie where her head rests on my shoulder.

"Yes, it is," I say, rubbing my hand across the back of my daughter's hair. She's been more subdued than normal this morning, and I worry there is something the doctors might have missed.

"No man in the picture to help you out with her raisin'?"

"Ah, no, Harmon," I say automatically.

Harmon is what the locals call a picker. He collects information about the passengers who ride in his cab and distributes it out to the rest of the county as he sees fit. Everybody knows if you don't want your business spread far and wide, then you don't share it with Harmon.

For the rest of the ride, I answer his questions with a polite yes or no. When he pulls up in front of the trailer a short while later, the look of disappointment on his face actually makes me feel guilty for not giving him even a morsel of gossip to share with his next passenger.

Harmon pulls Lexie's wheelchair from the trunk and sets it next to the back door. I slide out and then reach inside to lift Lexie up and put her gently in the seat. "How much, Harmon?" I ask, reaching inside my purse and pulling out my wallet.

"For you, five dollars, Miss Lila."

"Now that'll hardly pay for your gas."

"Five is good."

"Thanks, Harmon."

"You're surely welcome."

He gets back in the old red cab and pulls away with a wave out the window, and I feel guilty for not giving him a little more fodder for gossip.

I roll Lexie toward the trailer, glancing over at Rowdy's place where Brownie sits inside his sorry excuse for a doghouse. I hear his tail thump against the barrel side, but he doesn't get up and come out the way he usually does. "Hey, boy," I say.

The door to Rowdy's trailer opens, and Rowdy comes out with a chicken leg in each over-sized paw.

"About time you showed some manners," he throws Brownie's way, finishing off the remains of a leg and hurling the bone in Brownie's direction. The bone hits Brownie in the face. He yelps and retreats deeper inside the barrel.

"Chicken bones aren't good for dogs," I say, gripping the chair handles so hard I can feel my pulse pounding in my palms.

"What the hell you supposed to feed them then? Filet mignon?" he shoots back, giving both words a long "e" in a class-act effort to make them sound more French.

"The bones splinter in their throat," I say, dumb-ass in my tone if not in the actual words.

"Maybe that'll keep him from yappin' his mouth so much," Rowdy says with a big chuckle.

I hurry, wheeling Lexie toward the ramp leading to the trailer door.

"Awful lot of ruckus over here last night," Rowdy says in a louder voice. "And you not even here for your little girl when she needed you."

I let myself envision for a moment another fitting retribution for Rowdy, a severe case of food poisoning traced back to his bucket-a-day-fried-chicken habit. And maybe an internal parasite or two to boot.

♪

10

Lila

The Unexpected

Inside, the trailer is stifling hot. I turn on the air conditioning window unit, and then roll Lexie to her room. The doctor had recommended she rest for the remainder of the day, and I can see she needs it. Her eyes are heavy, and her shoulders droop. I pick her up and put her in bed, not bothering to change her clothes because she's still wearing her pajamas from last night.

Lexie snuggles under the covers and immediately falls asleep. I watch her, grateful for her soft, even breathing. I brush the back of my hand across her cheek, and she makes that snuffling noise I love to hear.

Lexie had been born six weeks early, and I'd been told she might not live out the week. Those first few days of her life, I never left her side. It's hard to explain the kind of bonding that happens when you're the only link between such a tiny being's survival and her succumbing to what's stacked against her.

Lexie had beaten the odds from day one, and every time I get scared like this, I remind myself my daughter is a fighter. She always pulls through. Always. This is just another temporary setback, and before long, she'll have that light in her eyes again.

I sit though for a long time, watching her sleep, until I no longer feel as if a pair of hands is at my throat. I get up finally and walk back to the kitchen to pour myself a glass of orange juice, taking long, thirsty gulps until it's gone. The fatigue hits me then, and I collapse on the living room couch, staring at the yellowed ceiling tiles.

The tears find their way up, sliding down my cheeks. I made a pact with myself the first time Lexie had one of her seizures that I would never again let her see me cry. She already has enough to be afraid of in this world.

But now, alone, I can't hold it back, and the sobs come out in great heaving gasps that don't have an ounce of dignity to them. I'm not proud of them. I hate giving in to weakness.

So I do what I always do. Get my song journal from

the bedroom and bring it back to the living room. I don't know where they come from, but the words are there, and I put them on the page, feeling better with each one. There is something in the making of a song that renews the will to fight inside me, bringing me back to a point where I can start swinging again.

Thoughts of last night fill my head, and I remember what it felt like to be in front of that crowd, singing a song I wrote. The only thing I can compare it to is what it felt like to spend the weekend at my grandma's house when I was a little girl, a safe haven for the time I was there, a place none of the hard stuff of regular life could touch. A place where my daddy didn't stripe my legs with a belt. A place where I could just be me, and that was okay.

That's what it had been like the night I first met Thomas in a downtown bar right before closing time when better judgment should have dictated that I head home. But I had been on the front row of the audience watching Thomas and Holden play, and it was so easy to lose myself in his voice, in the words of the songs he sang with such simple comfort. I don't think I moved throughout both of their sets. And when he made eye contact with me, giving me one of his wide, questioning smiles, I didn't look away.

When the show was over, and I reluctantly began

looking for Macy, the guy at the front door told me he'd seen her leave about an hour before with a guy in a Jeep. Since she had the car keys, there was nothing I could do except go outside and wait.

Thomas came out of the club exit door with three or four other guys, two of whom were complaining that it was too early for the place to shut down. One of them had looked at me and made a less than polite suggestion to join them in the back of somebody's truck for a continuation of the party.

Feeling uncomfortable, I got up and started walking away from the club. Thomas followed me and, when the others started after him, he'd turned around and told them to take off. The drunkest guy rattled out a protest along the lines of "So you get to have her all to yourself?"

"Get lost, boys," Thomas said, his tone no longer light. I had the feeling there was another phrase he would have preferred to use but refrained from doing so because of me.

The guys backed away, hands in the air, one of them muttering something about the singer always getting the girl.

I started walking again, even though I had no idea where to go.

"Hey," Thomas said. "I'll walk you to your car and make sure nobody else bothers you."

"Are you sure you're with them?" I'd asked.

"Not really," he said. "I got ditched by my buddy Holden for the girl he was hitting on in the front row."

I'd looked down and said, "I'm waiting on my friend. I'll be fine. Really."

"Where's your car?"

I pointed at the parking lot across the street. "Macy has the keys."

"Ah, dilemma," he said.

"Yeah."

"Can I get you a cab?"

"I actually live about an hour from here."

"Well, I'm staying at the Hotel Roanoke just across the bridge. Their bar might still be open. We could hang out there until she comes back."

"I don't think I need a bar," I said.

"Me either, actually," he agreed. "Coffee then, just until your friend comes back?"

That would have been the time to say no, make my way back to the bench until Macy returned with the car keys. But all it took was me letting myself meet his hopeful gaze to choose his company instead. A few minutes later, we were crossing the indoor bridge from downtown to the Hotel Roanoke.

Once we were inside the hotel, Thomas led the way to the Pine Room bar, but it had already closed.

We had both looked at each other a little awkwardly then. Thomas ran a hand across the back of his hair and said, "We can go up to my room and order some room service?"

Ordinarily, it would never have occurred to me to do anything remotely like that with someone I had just met, but he was nice, and it had been so long since I'd let anyone other than Macy past the walls I'd put up around myself.

Thomas led the way to the elevator, and we rode to the third floor in silence. At his door, he slipped the key in the lock and waved me inside. Jeans, T-shirts and a pair of running shoes littered the floor. He said sorry, embarrassed, and picked them up, opening the closet door and tossing them inside.

"I wasn't expecting company," he said.

"It's fine," I said.

He opened the minibar. "Cokes and stuff in here. Would you rather order coffee or–"

"Actually, Coke would be fine. Thanks."

He pulled out two, handed me one and then popped the tab on his. The soda bubbled up and sloshed out. He shook his head and grinned. "I'm not making much of an impression, am I?"

I smiled. "You're doing fine."

"You're being kind."

I shook my head and laughed a little. "When you were on that stage tonight, I'm pretty sure you could have picked any girl in the audience." I heard the flirtatious note in my voice and wondered where it had come from. When was the last time I had flirted with anyone?

He studied me for a moment, and then, serious, said, "There was only one I wanted."

I could hear the truth of it in his voice, even though it seemed a little hard for me to believe. I had watched him perform earlier with the absolute certainty that he would go on to big things. He had that kind of presence, that kind of voice. "Now you're being kind."

"I'm being honest."

We watched each other for a good long bit, just absorbing what it felt like to be this close, to want and wish.

I was the one who reached out first. My hand went to the side of his face, my palm encountering the rough stubble there, my thumb smoothing across his cheek.

I felt his sharp intake of breath, recognized it as a signal of my effect on him. It felt amazingly good to know that I could make him feel something. For a long time now, I had felt so little, and I wanted so badly to feel something real, something good.

He dipped his head towards mine, stopped just short of my mouth. I could feel the warmth of his breath on my lips, and I closed the distance between us, kissing him softly.

He put his hands on my waist, and I felt instantly anchored by him. As if I had been drifting on a stormy sea only to find myself in this peaceful harbor where I couldn't be turned upside down by circumstances out of my control.

He deepened the kiss and pulled me tight against him. I made a soft sound of relief that he wanted to hold me as much as I wanted him to.

We found our way to the bed, stretching out alongside each other, the light from the street below shining through the open curtain. We looked at each other, staring into each other's eyes without saying any words. We didn't need to.

Even then, I couldn't explain the connection between us. I just knew I felt it, knew I needed it. That no matter what it would mean beyond this night, I needed it.

I began to unbutton his shirt with shaking fingers. He stayed completely still while I worked my way to the very last one, pulling it out of his jeans and sliding my hands across the muscles in his back. I pulled him to me so that there wasn't an inch of space between us. That was when I felt the little collapse within him, felt him take the lead in where we would go from here. And I followed. Touch for touch. Kiss for kiss. Trying to give as much as I was taking. Relieved to know that I still had something to give.

Weeks later when I discovered that I was pregnant, I let myself play back every moment of it, closing my eyes and making myself remember it for what it had been. Something beautiful. Something at once temporary, and as it would turn out, lasting.

♪

11

Thomas

There Is a Tomorrow

When I get back to the hospital, Lila has already left with Lexie. I guess I shouldn't really be surprised, but it's plenty of evidence for the fact that Lila is no pushover. She's not going to let me into her life if I don't earn her trust first.

I take my time driving out to her place. I'm not sure if it's because I'm worried about my reception or if I'm starting to think I might be crazy to believe I can make a difference in either of their lives.

Since the shooting, and nearly being killed, I've pretty much chosen to live like there's no tomorrow. Because I know now that there might not be a tomorrow. Or a next hour. Or even a next minute. I haven't been making the smartest choices for somebody interested in living a long, fulfilling life.

I guess I've been trying to pack in as much living as I possibly could. But I'm starting to wonder if you can even call what I've been doing living at all. Really living, I mean.

I can't even remember the names of the girls I went out with a month ago. Seeing Lila and the commitment she's made to Lexie makes me realize I've been shallow and directionless.

Where the music is concerned, I've given that my all, and it's paid off. But as far as having someone in my life who really knows me, really cares about the me beneath the country music success, I don't have that.

So the truth is, right now, I'm not feeling too successful at all.

I wonder which me Lila sees. The one I've shown to the public or the one I showed her the night we spent together almost seven years ago.

With the exception of that night with Lila, the truth is I haven't shown that me to anyone else in the world except Holden and CeCe.

♪

WHEN I GET TO the trailer, the landlord's piece of crap truck is parked out front.

I decide to leave the stuff I've brought with me on the front seat until I make sure Lila and Lexie are here. I knock at the front door, then step back, swinging around to find the landlord glaring at me.

"If you're selling something," he says, "you're breaking the law. Didn't you see the 'No Soliciting' sign at the entrance?"

"I'm not selling anything," I say.

"Well if you ain't selling nothing, what are you doin' standing on the lady's porch?"

"Is that actually any of your business?" I ask with a narrow smile.

"Well, I'm the landlord of this here park. So I reckon it does, and if I walk over there and let my dog off its chain, you might wish you'd gotten in that truck of yours and left a little sooner."

The door to Lila's trailer opens, and she steps out, glancing from me to the landlord. "Rowdy, I don't recall anything in my lease stating I can't have visitors."

"Does this mean you want him in there? Or maybe you're just afraid I'll follow through on my threat to make Killer over there get off his hind end long enough to do some of the guard work he's supposed to be doing here anyway?"

"Come in, Thomas," Lila says, turning her back to Rowdy.

I follow her, closing the door behind us. "Is it even legal to be that much of a—"

"Jackass?" she finishes for me.

"Yeah," I say, "that."

"Unfortunately, I believe it is," she says. "No one has ever been out here to arrest him for it anyway."

"Maybe you ought to try reporting it."

She actually smiles a little at this.

"And Killer?"

"We call him Brownie. It's a name that actually fits him."

We're quiet for a moment, awkward, before I say, "How are you?"

"Okay."

"Lexie?"

"She's asleep."

A truck engine cranks up, and Lila goes to the window to glance out. "Good. He's leaving," she says.

"He doesn't seem like the most stable individual to live next to," I say, worry underscoring my words.

"I'm not scared of him."

"What if I'm scared for you?"

She looks up at me, her lips parting in surprise. "You don't need to be. He's just a big bag of hot air."

I shrug and nod a little, but I'm not sure I agree with her assessment that he's harmless.

"I brought a few things. Want to help me get them?"

"Sure," she says, shrugging and not quite meeting my gaze.

We walk out to the truck, and I open the door, reaching for the paper bag on the middle of the seat. "Maybe we should start with this before Napoleon gets back. I brought Killer a snack."

Lila's gaze widens. "Brownie?"

"Killer Brownie," I concede.

We walk over to the rusted barrel where Brownie sticks his head out, his tail thumping instantly at the sight of Lila. He whines softly and steps onto the dirt, the heavy chain attached to his collar clanking.

"Hey, Brownie," Lila says, dropping down onto her knees next to him.

The dog looks at me, cowering a little, uncertain.

"It's okay," Lila says, rubbing under his chin. "Look what he brought you."

I drop down next to her and pull a wrapper from the bag.

Brownie leans closer, sniffing with a hopeful tail wag.

"It's for you, boy," I say. "A Big Mac with no sauce. No pickle, lettuce, or tomato either. How's that sound?"

I break off a bite and hold it out to him. Brownie takes

it gently, as if he's not sure it's something to actually eat. But he swallows it and immediately asks for more.

"There you go," I say, handing him another bite and then feeding him one after another until it's all gone.

"He loved it," Lila says, rubbing under the dog's chin.

"Kinda wish I'd brought him more," I say.

"That was really nice of you," she says without looking at me. Her words are cautious, as if she's not quite sure it could be true.

"Not gonna make up for what he takes from that jerk though."

"I'm still hoping for spontaneous combustion or something," she says.

I smile at the unexpectedness of this from her. "Now there's a mental picture."

We sit and rub on Brownie for a few minutes before Lila stands and says, "I'd better check on Lexie."

I follow her inside the trailer, glancing over my shoulder just before I step inside. Brownie wags his tail, just a quick shake of the tip, as if he's not at all sure happiness can be trusted.

♪

12

Lila

He Loves Her

Lexie is awake when I go in her room. She smiles up at me, her blue eyes crinkling at the corners, and my heart melts just as it does every single time she smiles at me. I sit on the corner of her bed and smooth my hand across her silky blonde hair.

"Hi, sweet pea. Did you have a good nap?"

She nods, smiling at me and pulling the pink bunny she never sleeps without into the curve of her arm.

"There's someone I'd like for you to meet, sweetie."

She glances at the doorway and then back at me, and

I see the curiosity in her eyes. "He's waiting for us in the living room."

She scoots up in the bed the best she can, and I help her put her legs over the side, then pull her chair closer and lift her into it. Lexie loves company. She loves people, and every time I realize this, I wonder if I've sheltered her from the world too much. I've worried about what people will say to her, how it will make her feel, shape her self-image.

I worry now that Thomas won't think she's as perfect as I think she is.

With my heart clenching inside me, I roll her chair down the short hallway. Thomas is standing in the middle of the room with his hands in his pockets, worry clearly etched in his face. I understand suddenly that he is afraid she might reject him when I've been worrying about him rejecting her.

I stop the chair just short of where he's standing and lift her onto the couch. As I squat down beside her, I realize I have no idea what to tell her to call him. I look up at Thomas. He kneels down in front of her and holds out his hand. "Hi, Lexie. I'm Thomas. It's really nice to meet you."

She is slow to lift her hand to his, but she does so with deliberate effort. He takes it gently, and I can see him melt beneath her touch.

"She doesn't talk," I say in a soft voice. "But she understands everything you say to her."

Thomas nods once, reaching for the bag behind him. He slides it to her, and then pulls the edges open. She leans toward it and peers inside. She starts to flap her hands in the way that she claps, a big smile breaking across her face. Thomas reaches inside and pulls out an enormous stuffed toy.

"I used to have a Bassett Hound when I was growing up. I thought you might like this one."

He sets it down next to her, and Lexie rubs its soft ears. Her smile is all for Thomas.

"We could take him for a walk," I say.

Lexie looks at me, her eyes lit up.

"Would you like to do that?" I ask Thomas.

"Sure," he says.

I get Lexie's chair, and start to lift her into it, when Thomas says, "All right if I do that?"

I step back, and he picks her up as if she weighs no more than a feather, setting her on the wheelchair seat. He nestles the Bassett Hound in beside her, and I roll the chair to the door. He holds it open while I maneuver it onto the ramp.

"There's a fairly smooth path that we use to go for a walk. It leads down to the creek. It's pretty there."

"Sounds good," he says. "Lead the way."

We walk in silence for a minute or two, Lexie's chair making its whir-whir sound. She has the Bassett Hound clutched tightly to her chest, her cheek pressed against its head.

"I don't think you could have found anything she liked more."

"I wasn't sure what to get," he says, looking at me with relief.

I struggle to find the words for what I want to say and finally settle on just the honest truth. "I know where I live is a dump. You must think it's awful. It is awful."

"Lila," Thomas begins.

I interrupt him, needing to explain. "Just the deductible for Lexie's medical bills pretty much zaps my paychecks. I've needed to make that a priority. I've been able to save a little, and hopefully, we'll be able to move-"

"Lila," he says again, stopping me in a gentle voice. "I'm hardly in a position to judge you for anything. Not that I would anyway. But I could have helped make things easier. Made it so you didn't have to live in a place like this. Even if you didn't want me in your life. I would have done that for you both."

There's hurt in his voice, and yes, this surprises me. I'm not sure what to make of it. It's definitely not what I expected. But the realist in me prompts me to say, "I've seen the kind of life you lead in Nashville, Thomas. What would you do with this kind of responsibility? I didn't want to put that on you."

"You mean the kind of life the tabloids say I lead? I'm no saint, but then again I don't have the stamina to maintain what those losers say I'm up to."

I laugh a little, unexpectedly, the sound surprising us both. "That would definitely take some stamina."

He shakes his head, his expression hovering between disgusted and amused.

We walk on for a bit, and when he looks over at me, he is serious again. "Will you tell me about her, Lila? About when she was born? What happened and how you found out about the—"

"Cerebral palsy?"

He nods, and I can see it's hard for him to say the words. It use to be hard for me to say them. Until I was able to accept that they weren't a death sentence for Lexie.

We walk at a slow and even pace. Trees line either side of the wide path, shady shadows teasing us with streaks of sunlight.

"She was born at thirty-five weeks," I say, keeping my gaze focused straight ahead. Somehow, looking at him makes it hard for me to talk about it. "She weighed five pounds and was twenty inches long. Compared to some preemies, she didn't look premature at all. But her lungs weren't completely developed yet, and she wasn't strong enough to breastfeed."

"Is that why—"

He breaks off before finishing the question, but I know what he's asking. "The doctors don't know if the brain injury happened during pregnancy or afterward. Sometimes, I wish I knew, just to know whether it was something I did, or—"

Thomas reaches for my hand, slips it into his and squeezes hard. "Don't do that, Lila. I have no doubt that you did the best you could to take care of yourself and of her while you were pregnant. Just like you're doing now."

The words fill me with overwhelming gratitude. Tears spring to my eyes. Other people have said this to me before. But somehow, coming from him, maybe because he is half-responsible for her existence, I feel completely grateful.

"Thank you, Thomas."

"I should be the one thanking you. I don't know why things happened the way they did," he says. "Questioning it now seems like a waste. I think I'd rather choose to be grateful for the fact that you're both here and okay. And hope that you'll give me a chance to make things a little easier for you."

"I don't expect anything from you, Thomas."

"I think you've made that pretty obvious," he says.

We stop at the end of the path where the edge of the creek begins. Lexie points at the big rock in the middle of the water that I've carried her out to many times.

"Lexie likes to sit there in the sun," I say, looking up at Thomas.

"Looks like a good place to me," he says. "All right if I take her out?"

"Sure," I say.

We lean down and take off our shoes, then roll up our jeans. I unbuckle the belt on Lexie's chair and step back so he can lift her up.

She looks into his face and smiles. He smiles back at her, and the resemblance they share makes me wonder how I could ever have thought he didn't deserve to know his daughter. Or that he might reject her.

"Lead the way," he says, glancing at me, his eyes bright with something I don't remember seeing in them until now. Like when someone has discovered something that was supposed to be a part of them all along.

♪

13

Thomas

The Day We Met

I stay until dark. Lila makes us something to eat, but I'm not hungry. I feel full with something not quite like anything I've ever felt before. It's this satisfaction, this completeness that I feel every time I look at Lila and Lexie.

When she indicates that it's Lexie's bedtime, I stand to leave, wishing I didn't have to go. Lila walks me to the door, and we step out onto the porch.

I look at her for a few moments, absorbing her pretty face, the light in her eyes that's been there since this afternoon at the creek.

"Thanks for letting me come," I say.

"I should thank you for coming."

I rake a hand through my hair, draw in a deep breath and blow it out slowly. "Lila. We need to figure out where to go from here."

"I don't expect anything from you, Thomas."

"You should."

"But I don't."

I study the deliberate blankness in her expression, asking, "Who let you down so badly? Other than me, I mean."

"You didn't let me down. I never gave you a chance to do the right thing."

I start to deny it, but we both know it's true. "Who then?"

She walks over to lean against the porch railing, propping herself up with both elbows. She stares out into the encroaching night, and it's a long time before she says anything.

"When I was a senior in high school, I came home from school one afternoon with Macy. We were going to work on an English project. We were laughing when we walked through the front door. I don't even remember at what now. Something silly. Meaningless. My mom almost always came out to give me a kiss when I got home from school. But she didn't that day. And she didn't answer when I called her even though her car was in the driveway."

I have a sudden feeling of dread in my stomach, and I want to stop her. Tell her I don't want to hear the rest, but I don't. I can't.

"We found her on the living room floor," Lila says, her voice now barely audible. "There was so much blood. I never knew one person could hold that much blood. And she was so pale, her beautiful skin this pasty, chalky, unearthly white."

Lila is completely still, her gaze on something far away that I cannot see. I want to say something, but I can't force out a single word. I feel like I've been thrown back to the night of the shooting, to the moment when the shooter pointed his gun at me, and I knew he was going to pull the trigger.

"I dropped to my knees because all the air left me," Lila says. "I crawled to her. It felt as if my legs weighed a thousand pounds each, and I could barely pull them behind me. I draped myself across her, trying to match her shape with my own as if I could infuse her with my own life, but my clothes just soaked up her blood."

"My God. Lila." I want to tell her to stop, that she doesn't have to go on. But I can see that she needs to, and so I stay quiet.

"I don't remember what happened over the next couple

of days. I guess the doctors at the hospital gave me something that made me sleep, so I basically missed the torturous necessities of removing my mom's body from the house, cleaning up all the blood, and arresting my dad.

"When I finally came home from the hospital, there wasn't one speck of evidence that any of it had ever happened. Our living room was just as it had always been. I fully expected her to call out from the kitchen, 'Cookies in the oven. Do you want milk with yours?' Her voice was so real to me that I ran around the house looking for her, sure that all of it had been a nightmare of some kind and that she wasn't really gone."

"Lila," I say. "Stop. You don't have to tell me anymore."

"I want you to know. I think I need for you to know," she says, hesitating. And then, "I ended up staying in a psychiatric hospital for six weeks. The goal, the doctors said, was to basically protect me from myself, give me time come to terms with what had happened. I hated every single drug-numbed moment I spent there. I wanted to feel it, all of it, the rage and the all-consuming sadness. My mother deserved to be mourned."

Her shoulders start to shake. I reach out and pull her to me, banding her against my chest as if I can absorb the pain she is feeling.

"That's when I met you," she says. "I had just gotten out of the hospital that day."

I try to take this in, but I can't seem to get any of it to process. "And I was—"

"Comfort," she says. "You didn't know. And I needed you. So actually, I guess it was me taking advantage of you, if we're both truthful."

I hold her tight against me, while the night sounds start up. A whippoorwill somewhere behind us. The frogs at the creek where we'd walked earlier today.

"Your dad?" I finally ask. "What happened?"

"He's in prison. Life without chance of parole."

"Lila. Dear God," I say against her hair, wishing I had words, any words, that would actually mean something in light of everything she's just told me. "All this time, have you had anyone? Any family?"

"Macy. And her mom. They're like family to me."

I hold her as long as she'll let me. I want to absorb her pain, every speck of it so that she never has to feel it again. "How did you make it through all of that, Lila? I can't imagine—"

"Most of the time we're stronger than we think," she says softly. "I suspect you already know that, though."

"Yeah," I say, realizing she's talking about the shooting. "I wanted to tell you how sorry I was for what happened to all of you, but I thought you might not want to talk about it."

"It's okay," I say. "I don't think it'll ever be easy, but I'm in a different place from the one I was in a year ago."

"I'm glad you had your friends to be there for you."

"We've been there for each other. And yeah, I don't know what I would have done without them." I hesitate and then say, "I wish I had known what happened to you, Lila."

"But you didn't. And I didn't want you to. I just wanted that night to be what it was. An escape."

"It turned out to be a lot more than that, didn't it?"

"It did. But I don't question it. I can't imagine my life without Lexie, Thomas. In most ways, I think she saved me. Gave me a reason to go on."

I nod once, feeling the truth of this, even as I realize I don't quite know how to process it all, weave it together in my head. I just know that like Lila, I can't question what happened between us now. Or her decision to keep Lexie from me. Somehow I think I know that if I had been her, I would have done the same thing.

When she finally pulls away from me, I feel her emotional withdrawal in addition to the physical.

"I have to get Lexie to bed," she says.

"Can I come back tomorrow, Lila?"

She looks away, considers the question for several moments, as if doubting the wisdom of telling me yes.

I tip her chin up with one finger, forcing her to meet my eyes. "Please?"

"Okay," she says, stepping back. "Goodnight, Thomas."

"Goodnight, Lila."

When the door closes, I walk out to the truck and get inside. It's only then that I allow the knot in my chest to find relief through the tears that slide down my face.

I look at the sorry excuse for a doghouse Brownie is tied to. He's sitting outside of it, watching me. I wish I could walk over there, unhook him and put him in the truck with me, get him away from that sorry excuse for a human he belongs to.

It sucks to be a victim.

♪

14

Lila

Not Just About Me

It's after eleven o'clock when I hear the knock at the door. I get out of bed and pull the living room curtain back to see Macy's car parked outside.

She's in mid-knock when I undo the deadbolt and let her in.

"Girl, don't you ever answer your phone?"

"Sorry. I let the battery die."

"And how am I supposed to know you're okay?" she asks, walking over to the couch and plopping down with an accusatory glare. "How is Lexie? I've been worried sick about her."

"She's okay," I say. "She's asleep. What are you doing out so late? We have to work tomorrow."

"I couldn't go to sleep without knowing the two of you were all right."

"Sorry, Mace," I say, contrite now.

"I smell expensive cologne," she says.

"I don't smell anything."

"Thomas was here, wasn't he?" she says, sitting up with an ah-ha smile.

"So what if he was?"

"So *everything* if he was. What happened? I want to hear all."

"Macy. Please don't start making something out of this that it's not going to be."

"You're the one who needs to make something out of it."

"I don't want anything from him."

"You're not the only one involved, Lila. Not trying to be mean here, but you've got Lexie to think of. And God knows, you need help."

"We're doing fine."

"You call this doing fine?" she asks, throwing a hand in the air.

"I didn't say it was the Taj Mahal."

"That it isn't. Plus that creep Rowdy next door. He gives me the heebies."

"He's harmless. Gross, but harmless."

"Lila?"

"Yeah?"

"Don't let pride talk you out of letting Thomas in. I know how hard it is for you to accept anything from anyone, but it's time you changed that."

I want to argue with her, but I'm too tired, and I drop onto the sofa next to her. She slides over and puts her head on my shoulder. "I love you. You've got to quit being so dang tough."

"It's gotten me through so far," I say, trying to sound lighthearted but hearing my own failure.

"Just the fact that he came over here must mean something."

"He wanted to meet Lexie."

"I don't doubt that a bit. And why wouldn't he? You never gave him a chance to be a stand-up guy. You know I love you, girl, but I've never thought that was fair to him or to Lexie."

"If you thought I was so wrong, why are you just now saying it?"

"Truth?"

"Truth."

"I was afraid he might be a jerk and reject you both. I don't think I could stand to see you go through another horrible thing that you don't deserve."

I reach out and put my hand over hers.

"But he hasn't," Macy says. "Rejected you, I mean."

"Yet."

"You doubt his sincerity?"

"I think he wants to help. What exactly that means, I'm not sure. What if Lexie gets attached to him and then he decides—"

"If we play the what-if game," Macy interrupts, "we'll just sit here and depress ourselves into a stupor. You've gotta give him a chance, Lila."

"Be real. He's got this life in Nashville that has in no way included having a daughter."

"Yeah, so he's a player. You could change all that."

"Right."

"You could."

"Have you seen some of the girls he goes out with?"

"They airbrush everybody in those magazines," Macy says, dismissing my concern with a wave of her hand. "You can't tell me that he didn't take one look at our Lexie and fall in love."

I'd like to deny it, but I can't. I had seen the look in his eyes. Watched the transformation on his face. "No. I can't."

"So let it happen, Lila. Let it happen for Lexie, if not for you."

♪

15

Thomas

I Have a Daughter

I call Holden on the way back to the hotel. He answers on the first ring.

"What up?"

"Got a minute?"

"Sure. I'm fixing dinner. CeCe's upstairs taking a bath."

"And you're not up there with her?" I crack.

"Not yet," he comes back, and I hear the grin in his voice.

I release a long breath, not sure where to start.

"Something wrong?" he asks, concern edging out the humor now.

"I don't know if you'd call it something wrong or something right," I say.

"Don't tell me you finally found a woman who'd have you and eloped?"

"Shut up."

"If not that, then what?"

"I have a daughter."

Silence hangs on the line for several moments before Holden says, "Did you just say you have a daughter?"

"I did say that."

"Thomas. What the. . ."

"It's Lila."

"Wait. Are you telling me you and Lila have a daughter?"

"Yeah."

"Are you serious, Thomas. How?"

"The usual way, dumb ass."

Holden barks a short laugh. "You know what I mean."

"That one night. She had a baby."

"And never told you?"

"No."

"Whoa. How did you find out?"

"I found out she left the show because her daughter had been taken to the hospital. I went by to see if they were all right. Turns out her daughter is also my daughter."

"Did she tell you that?"

"She didn't have to tell me. All I had to do was look at her."

"Damn."

"Yeah."

"I guess that's why she blew you off so badly, huh?"

"I guess."

"So what are you going to do now?"

"I want to help her out."

"Lila or the little girl?"

"Her name is Lexie. And both."

"What exactly does that mean? Both."

"That's the part I haven't figured out yet."

"Man, don't get in over your head. You don't really even know her."

"Aren't you the white knight?"

"I just don't want to see you get taken advantage of."

"She lives in a friggin' trailer park, Holden. With this ass-wipe of a landlord who looks at her like he wants to eat her for lunch."

"That ain't good."

"I want to get them out of there. I have to get them out of there."

"And bring them here?"

"I don't know. Maybe. I've barely got any of this straight in my head yet. It seems like we need a little time to sort things through here."

Holden is quiet for a few seconds, before saying, "Remember that lake we went to the afternoon before the show? Smith. . ."

"Mountain," I finish for him.

"Yeah. That's it. I think I remember hearing that people rent houses out there. Maybe you could get a temporary place there."

I instantly like the idea. "That might be good."

"How long will you stay?"

"I'm not sure."

"We've got the tour for the new album coming up next month. We're gonna need you in rehearsals."

"I know. Just give me a few days, okay."

"Want us to come down there?"

"No," I say. "At least, not yet."

"You know we'll leave tonight if you say the word."

"I appreciate that. And yeah, I know."

"What's she like? Lexie?"

"Beautiful," I say. "Sweet." I don't add the rest because I don't feel ready to share it. And it's not that I'm ashamed of her. I guess the word would be more like protective. I don't want Holden to form an impression of her that doesn't include experiencing her smile, the light in her eyes.

"Send us pictures."

"I will. Hey, thanks, man. For the talk."

"You don't ever need to thank me for being there for you, Thomas. It's just the way it is. And always gonna be."

We talk music and work for a few minutes, and when I finally click off the call, I realize Holden has always been more brother to me than friend. I'm grateful he's in my life. Right now, I can use both.

♪

16

Lila

On a White Horse

Bertha and Marsha are in rare form this morning.

They've somehow gotten wind of my performance on my birthday, and they're reaching new highs in the department of ridicule.

Bertha leans over the conveyor belt so that she's right in front of my face when she sneers, "If you can sing so good, Miss Extra-ordinary, why you still workin' at Smart-Send? You hopin' they'll hire you to yodel their commercials for them?"

"I'm still holding out hope, Bertha," I say, without meeting her gaze. I could tell her that she might want to take a closer look at her dental hygiene practices, but I refrain.

"That would be something," her sidekick Marsha offers from her spot just up the line. "Head Yodeler for Smart-Send. Every girl's dream come true."

I keep my gaze on the box in front of me, fold the edges in and seal them with my tape gun.

"Aw, now we ain't done hurt your feelings, have we?" Bertha says, blowing another whoosh of bad breath my way.

I lean back and stay quiet.

"What?" Marsha jabs. "You playin' the mouse this morning since Mother Macy ain't here to defend you?"

"Any particular reason she might need defending?"

Surprise jolts through me. Thomas walks toward us, a ball cap pulled low on his head. It is completely ineffective as a disguise. I feel everyone around us looking at him. "What are you doing here?"

"Visiting you," he says.

"But you're not supposed to be back here in the factory."

He smiles at me with the very same smile that caused me to end up having his baby.

"Turns out the receptionist likes country music."

"Ah," I say.

Bertha throws me a glare and then narrows her gaze at Thomas. "You with that Barefoot Outlook band?"

"I am," he says, his smile now wary.

"So what are you doin' in a place like this?" she asks, waving a pudgy hand at our surroundings.

"Here to see a girl," he says, eyes narrowed as if he's decided to play along for a bit.

"That girl?" Bertha asks, pointing at me.

"That girl," he agrees.

She considers this and looks at me. "Only one reason I can think of for a girl like our Miss Lila to get a dude like you in a place like this. And that makes her way smarter than I ever gave her credit for."

"You get yourself knocked up, Lila?" Marsha jumps in.

I feel the flush in my face, the heat as it scalds my cheeks. I grapple for a response, but can't make one come out.

Bertha snorts and shakes her head, her extra chin jiggling as she does. "Well, let's just hope he was able to give you one that's not damaged like that one you got now."

The air around us goes completely still. I feel Thomas's rage bubbling up. Just as I move to step between him and Bertha, he body slams her against the conveyor belt, his hands out at his sides as if he is forcing himself not to wrap them around her neck.

"This how you get your kicks all day long? You're a class act, you know it? Be glad you're not a man, or I'd already have you taped up and riding this assembly line to that truck waiting on the other end."

Her eyes narrow to ugly slits, her voice venomous when she says, "You lay a hand on me, and I'll file enough charges against you to wipe out your fat Nashville bank account."

"Thomas, stop!" I say, ducking under the machine to grab his arm and try to pull him away. "It's not worth it."

"If I ever lay a hand on you, ma'am," he says, still glaring down at Bertha, "you'll sure as heck know it. You breathe one more word about my daughter, and I'm not making you any promises. We clear?"

She lifts her flabby chin in defiance, but for the first time ever, manages not to say anything.

Thomas steps back, as if he can't stand another moment that close to her. He reaches for my hand and says, "Come on."

"I can't leave now, Thomas. I'll be fired."

He pulls me along behind him as if I weigh nothing at all. "They can't fire you. You quit."

"I don't quit," I say. "I can't!"

He turns and looks down at me. "You don't need this place. You don't need that," he says with a pointed glare back at Bertha.

"I do need this paycheck."

"Not anymore."

"Thomas. You can't just come in here and upend my life! It might not be much, but it's what I've got."

"You deserve more."

"What does that have to do with reality?" I ask, suddenly furious at him for sparking in me a desire for more, for something I gave up hope of a long time ago.

"I'm not leaving you here with that crazy—"

"You don't have a choice!" I say, turning abruptly and heading for my spot on the assembly line.

But he's way faster than I am, and before I even realize what he's doing, he's swooped me up in his arms and is striding back down the aisle. Clapping sounds all around us.

"Yay, Lila!" someone yells from behind us.

"Get on out of here while you've got the chance!"

Whistling accompanies the clapping.

I struggle to slip out of his arms, but that's not happening.

At the end of the assembly line, Thomas stops and turns around, still holding me in his arms. "Oh, and ma'am?" he calls back to Bertha. "You might want to try out this new invention called a toothbrush."

♪

17

Thomas

Conduct Becoming

I don't put her down until we reach my truck in the parking lot. When I finally do, she is so mad I think she might take a swing at me.

"What are you doing?" she screams, forcing her hands into fists at her side.

"Something you probably wouldn't ever do for yourself."

"What does that mean?" she throws back, her eyes shooting fire.

"Making you leave that place. Is that what you think

you deserve? Being treated like that every single day by that witch in polyester?"

"I never said it was about what I deserve! I *need* the paycheck!"

"No, you don't."

"Yes, I do!" she yells.

I walk around to the front of the truck, leaning against the hood and folding my arms across my chest. "When you cool off, we'll talk."

"When *I* cool off?"

"Yeah."

"Has your ego really been nursed to these proportions by all those fans of yours? That you think you can just come in here and smash to smithereens everything I've done to take care of Lexie?"

"It doesn't have anything to do with ego, Lila. She's my daughter too."

"Yeah, and I have no idea what you're going to think about that in a week, a month. If you're going to get tired of responsibility and start longing for your playboy life? You're not a sure thing, Thomas! Lexie and I need a sure thing. What I've built for us here might not be much, but it is a sure thing. *Was* a sure thing until you messed it up!"

"Lila—" I start, but she's turning for the factory and marching across the parking lot to the main entrance.

I go after her, blocking her path and forcing her to

stop. "Give me a chance," I say. "I know you have no reason on earth to believe this, but if you'll just put your trust in me, I promise I won't let you down."

Tears well in her eyes and slide down her cheeks. She wants to believe me. I can see that she does. But I don't have any other words to convince her with. The only thing that's going to do that is time.

I step out of her way, giving her the choice of going back. I realize now I can't make her do this. It has to be her choice.

She looks at the door to the factory. She looks at me.

I hold out my hand.

We stand here this way long enough that I'm pretty sure she's going back inside. When she starts walking toward the door, my heart drops in my chest. I can't bring myself to say her name.

I force myself to turn and start walking to the truck, my steps heavy.

But then I hear her running toward me, and I don't look back. I just hold out my hand. And she takes it.

♪

18

Lila

Say Yes

We don't say anything for the first five minutes after we pull away from the factory. Thomas just drives, and I stick my head out the window, letting the wind blow my hair straight back.

I feel like I've been set free, but even as I acknowledge this, I know what I've just done is bona-fide crazy.

I finally sit back in the seat and look over at him. "I can't let you take care of me," I say. "I have to be able to take care of myself."

He doesn't answer for a moment, and when he does,

his voice is full of understanding. "I never thought you would. But you can let me help."

"I have to have a job."

"You have an incredible voice, Lila. What about that?"

"I appreciate that, Thomas. But it's not a job."

"It could be."

"I've been away from music a long time."

"When it's in you, I don't think it ever leaves you."

I want to deny this, but I can't. I've never stopped loving writing songs. Even when I knew I'd never sing them out loud for anyone but myself.

A tidal wave of anxiety washes over me. "This is nuts, Thomas."

"We have very different lives. In very different places. And you have a full life with your career. How often are you actually going to want to visit here?"

He taps his thumb on the steering wheel, and I can see that he's nervous, as if he's trying to get up the courage to say something he's having trouble saying. "What would you think about moving to Nashville? You and Lexie, I mean?"

The question takes me so by surprise that I can only stare at him, sure I must have heard him wrong. "What?"

"I know it sounds like a huge step, but you're right. It would be hard for me to get here as often as I'd want to. With you there. . .we have a great children's hospital at

Vanderbilt. And your music . . . you could work on that. I could hook you up with some producers for demo work right away. That would give you an income while you work on your own stuff. I mean, I know it's important to you to be independent."

"Wow," I say, letting out a long breath. "I don't know what to say."

"Just say yes. And we'll make it happen."

"It's really that simple for you, isn't it?"

"This is. Yeah. I want to know my daughter, Lila. Is that so wrong?"

I shake my head, not trusting my voice to answer him. "I don't want to keep you from her, Thomas. But I don't know if I can do what you're asking."

"Why not?"

I shrug, unable to find the exact words. "I just. . .I guess I'd gotten to a place of acceptance where my life is concerned. That some things aren't going to turn out the way I once hoped they would. My consolation has been Lexie. No dream I ever had compares to what I have in her."

"I can see that," he says. "I'm grateful that you're her mother, Lila. I mean that. I'm not proud to admit this, but I've known some girls who would never be the kind of mother you've been."

"Thank you," I say. "That actually means a lot to me."

"I'd like to pay you back, Lila, in whatever way I can. In whatever way you'll let me."

"You know I don't expect that."

"I know."

We drive for a few minutes before I force myself to say, "If any of this actually happens, our connection with each other will be as parents to Lexie. This doesn't mean there will be any kind of romantic thing between us."

"No," he says, quickly enough that I wonder if he's glad I'm getting this out of the way.

"You probably already have a girlfriend. Girlfriends," I correct. "And I don't want to get in the middle of any of that."

"As a matter of fact, I'm currently unattached, but I appreciate the concern," he says with some irony.

"And I. . ."

"Will of course be free to date whoever you want to."

"Of course."

"Is there. . .anybody in the picture?"

"No one serious," I say, trying to sound as if that could change at any moment.

"Lila. I know it's a lot to think about. But give me a chance, okay? We'll take it one day at a time. Figure out how to make all this work. I've rented a house at the lake for a week. Would you and Lexie come out and stay with me there a few days? So we could all spend a little time together?"

I feel myself falling farther and farther down this rabbit hole. Alarm skitters through me when I think of all the potential hazards along the way. How very likely it is that Thomas will eventually yearn for the life he had before Lexie and me.

But a few days at the lake sounds so wonderful that I cannot bring myself to say no. I can only imagine how much Lexie will love it.

And so I nod. Once. And then look back out the window.

♪

19

Thomas

All it Takes

I get to the trailer the next morning at nine. I'll admit I didn't sleep hardly any all night. I kept thinking Lila would call and say she'd changed her mind. That she didn't think spending a week with me was a good idea.

Not that I would blame her.

I've basically turned her life upside down, and I just hope I'm doing it for all the right reasons.

I knock at the door, looking over my shoulder where Brownie is curled up inside his barrel-house. I think about Hank Junior and Patsy. The life they have with

CeCe and Holden. And it seems so damn unfair that this dog is never going to know that kind of care and love.

Lila opens the door, notices the direction of my gaze and says, "I'm just gonna steal him one day."

"Definitely be the best thing that ever happened to him."

"If I didn't think I'd be the first person Rowdy would accuse, I'd do it today."

"Think he'd sell him?"

"I've already tried that. He's offended that I don't think this life is good enough for him."

"Ass."

"Yeah," she says.

I notice how she looks then, the jean shorts that show off her long legs and suddenly have me remembering the feel of them wrapped around me. Awareness must register on my face because she backs inside and clears her throat.

"I was just finishing up getting Lexie's things."

"Take your time," I say, my voice a little uneven. "No hurry."

"She's in her room. Want to say hi and help her get in her chair?"

"Yeah. That'd be great."

"Go ahead," she says, smiling softly.

I walk down the short hall, stopping in the doorway of

her room. She's sitting on the bed, playing with the Basset Hound toy I had given her. He appears to be having a conversation with her bunny.

"Hey, Lexie. How are you?"

She looks up at me and smiles, a full, happy smile that tells me she's glad to see me. My heart does a flip and then ties itself in a knot. "Your mama tell you we're going to the lake?"

She makes a swimming motion with one arm.

"You like the water?"

Another nod, her smile now a little shyer than it was at first.

"We're gonna have us some big-time fun," I say.

She scoops the bunny up under one arm, the Basset Hound under the other. I can see that it's not easy for her to hold onto them, but she manages.

"All right if I carry you out to your chair?"

She nods again, her smile sweet and happy, indicating I'll need to pick up all three of them.

And I melt. That's all there is to it. I just melt.

♪

20

Lila

Glass Houses

You know how you can be having a dream right before you wake up in the morning? And you're aware that it's a dream, but it's so good you don't want to open your eyes? You just want it to keep going?

That's what it feels like when we pull up in front of the house Thomas has rented at Smith Mountain Lake.

"This is incredible," I say.

"I thought it would be nice for everything to be on one level," he says, glancing back at Lexie, who is looking at the big house with awe in her eyes.

"That was really thoughtful," I say.

The center of the house is glass so that you can see right through the middle to the lake view on the other side. A ski boat pulls a skier across the smooth surface. A pontoon boat motors lazily along in the distance.

"Thomas, this is too much," I say, finding my voice.

"You don't like it?" he asks, instantly worried.

"No, it's not that. It's just. . .we're not use to things like this." The part I don't say is that deep down I'm worried that being here will make Lexie see our real life as it truly is: unable to compare.

But I know that's selfish. I don't want to deny her this experience. And so I look at Thomas and smile. "It's amazing. Really. Thank you."

"Let's go see if it lives up to its billing," he says, getting out of the truck. He gets Lexie's chair from the back and walks around to her side, opening the door and unbuckling her seat belt. She holds her arms out to him, and my heart does a little flip at the way in which she is already bonding with him.

Part of me is really happy about that. Another part of me, the insecure part, worries that she will start to see me as less.

Thomas rolls Lexie's chair along the sidewalk to the front door, fishing the keys out of his pocket. He unlocks it and swings it open, waving me ahead of them. "You first," he says.

I step into the foyer and stare, at a loss for words.

The glass on this side of the house runs the width of the enormous living room so that it looks like the surface of the lake is within reach. Sunlight glints diamonds across the stretch of blue-green water.

Oversize chairs face the view, and I think I could sit there all day long, just taking it in.

"I've never seen anything so beautiful," I say, finally finding the words.

Thomas puts his hand on my shoulder, squeezes once. "Let's just enjoy it," he says. "I'll get our things out of the truck. You check everything out."

I roll Lexie over to the glass door that leads out onto the deck, open it, and we're outside, a light breeze lifting our hair, the sun warm on our skin.

Lexie makes a sound of delight, pointing at a parasail in the distance. We watch as it glides through the air, high above everything down here. That's kind of how I feel right now, like I've been granted a temporary view of something normally out of my reach.

A few minutes later, Thomas joins us on the deck. He leans forward with his elbows on the railing. "It's so peaceful," he says.

"I've lived in this county my whole life and barely ever seen this lake. I had no idea it was so beautiful."

He looks at me then, our gazes holding. I see in his

eyes a mixture of things I'm not sure I want to take apart and identify. I don't want his pity. Of anything I could possibly ever want from him, it's not that.

"So here's what I propose," he says, his voice low and persuasive. "For the next few days, there's just this and the three of us. No past. No future. Just the present. Can we do that?"

I have no idea how to do that, but I know that I want to. I really want to. "Yes," I say. "We can."

♪

21

Thomas

It's the Simple Stuff

We spend the afternoon motoring around the lake on the pontoon boat that came with the house rental.

I've never driven a boat before, so there's a good deal of figuring out as we go. How to get it out of the hanging slip. Where the lifejackets are stored. How to accelerate without giving us all whiplash. My novice efforts result in a good bit of laughter on Lila's part, and just the sound of it makes my bumbling worth it.

Smith Mountain Lake is enormous with more than five hundred miles of shore line. We're staying near the center where the widest part flows out beneath its namesake, a beautiful green flow of mountain that reminds me of Lake Como in Italy where my mom had taken me when I'd graduated from high school.

I find a cove at the foot of the mountain and anchor the boat. There's not another boat in sight.

Lila is stretched out on one of the front seats, her face to the sun. Lexie is playing with some toys on the floor under the covered part of the boat.

I beach the pontoon on a strip of sand and look at Lila, trying to keep my gaze on her face, which takes no small amount of willpower considering that she's wearing a blue bikini that leaves little to the imagination. Not that I need to imagine. I remember.

"This look like a good spot to swim?" I ask.

She sits up on the seat, taking in the view. "It's perfect," she says. "Lexie? Do you want to swim?"

Her smile is the only answer we need.

She's wearing a life jacket with a strap between the legs for extra security. Lila picks her up and walks to the front of the boat.

I slide off into the water, my feet hitting the bottom instantly.

Lila leans down and hands Lexie to me and says, "I'll get the floats."

Lexie's face is lit with happiness. She hits the water with one hand, giggling when it splashes on me. I drop into the water until it reaches her shoulders, and she's laughing now, flicking the water at me.

Lila hops in next, sliding a float my way. She climbs on the other, lying face down, her chin on her arm, watching us. "She loves water," she says.

"I can see that." I lift her up and set her on my shoulders. For the next little bit, we play shark with Lila and King of the Mountain. And at times, Lexie is laughing so hard, she can barely catch her breath.

I think about all the things I've done in my life so far that have given me satisfaction. There have actually been quite a few. Playing college football. Starting a band with Holden. Moving to Nashville and carving out a career there. Our first concert tour. All of it was great, and I'm thankful for every moment of it.

But I can honestly say, carting this little girl around on my shoulders while she makes her mama laugh, none of it compares to this.

♪

22

Lila

Awareness

I guess I never let myself imagine what Thomas would be like as a father. If I had, I don't think I would have done him justice.

He talks to her and not at her, as I've noticed so many adults doing. And she hangs on his every word. Her eyes follow him as if she can't wait to see what he does next.

On that score, I can surely identify with her. I swear, he looks like he could be one of those models for Abercrombie and Fitch. The ones on the life-size posters outside their stores. He's wearing swim shorts that hang low on his hips. His abs are cut. Ditto for his chest and biceps. I'm taking all of this in one stolen glance at a time.

I've pretty much gotten away with a full-body appraisal when he catches me dead on, his gaze snagging mine and forcing me not to look away.

Lexie is on his shoulders, and he's got his arms stretched out wide, holding her hands in his. He returns my visual assault, starting with my face and then letting his gaze drop with deliberate acknowledgment of what he's taking in.

He says nothing, but he doesn't need to.

I feel my face go bright red. I bite my lower lip and then quickly wipe the back of my hand across my mouth in case he took that as an invitation of some sort.

I'm not sure how long we stand there, staring at each other, but it's long enough that my heart is beating so hard in my chest that I can feel it in my ears. I do the only thing I can think to do to douse the fire that has erupted inside me.

I sink into the water until it completely covers my head.

Even so, I can still hear Thomas's soft laughter.

♪

WE SPREAD QUILTS ON the sandy shore and eat the sandwiches Thomas made for us.

Lexie's is peanut butter and jelly. Ours tomato and

Havarti cheese with some kind of basil mayo that is just downright yummy.

"And you cook too," I say, taking a sip of my bottled water.

"Not sure this actually qualifies, but I can make some pretty mean sandwiches," he says.

He's also brought along some kind of brownie with pink icing on top.

"I don't know who's happier," I say. "Lexie or me."

"Who doesn't love brownies?" he asks, taking a bite and then licking a morsel of chocolate from his lower lip. I find myself wishing I could do that for him. No sooner has the thought crossed my mind than I feel my face heat up again, and I look away, aware that he can probably read every lascivious thought I'm having.

"Tell me about your music," he says out of the blue.

I look at him, surprised. I shrug. "There's really not much to tell these days."

"Macy said you've kept writing. That you never stopped."

"It's just a part of my day."

"I'd love to hear some of your songs."

"I don't think they're up to your standards," I say.

"Say what?"

"I mean, you've got one of the best writers in Nashville creating your stuff."

"Well, I agree Holden is as good as they get. But he's been writing his whole life, too. Just like you."

"He's got a gift."

"He does. Macy says you do, too. I know that voice of yours is a gift."

"Thanks, Thomas. But Macy is a little biased."

"Hey, we all need someone in our corner. That girl's got your back and then some."

"There have been times in my life when I don't know what I would have done without her."

"Play me a few songs tonight, after Lexie goes to bed?"

"I don't know," I say, shaking my head. "I'm not sure I can."

"Why not?"

"Because you make me nervous."

"I make you nervous?"

"Yeah," I say, trying not to smile. "You do."

"You got any idea why?"

"Not really."

He laughs his low, sexy laugh.

And I think he has a very, very good idea why.

♪

WE LEAVE THE wonderful spot at the foot of Smith Mountain and head over to a nearby marina to put gas in the boat.

The young guy who greets us at the pump jumps in to

remove the gas cap, smiling at Lexie who waves a small hand at him.

"Bet you haven't seen our fish," he says to her.

"We haven't," says Thomas, stepping into the conversation.

"She'll love it," he says, pointing to the back of the small metal building that apparently houses the marina's snack bar. "They like popcorn. You can get that inside."

"Thanks," Thomas says, picking up Lexie and following me off the boat.

We buy three bags of popcorn inside from a very nice lady who recognizes Thomas the moment we walk in the door.

"Well, my goodness," she says. "You're Thomas Franklin with—" she shakes her hand as if that will jar her memory for the name. "Barefoot Outlook!"

He smiles at her, looking a little awkward, and I realize he's never really gotten use to this part. But then I wonder if you ever do. She asks him to autograph one of the marina ball caps and thanks us for coming in.

We walk around to the back of the building and onto a dock. Hundreds of fish swim in a circle, their mouths pointed upward at us, lips opening and shutting in a silent request for us to share our popcorn.

Lexie points at them and makes cooing sounds of joy. Thomas opens a bag for her, and she sticks her hand inside, showering the fish with it. They begin flapping, all in the same quest to get the treat. Thomas upends the rest of the bag, and they flap harder. Lexie laughs in pure delight.

The three of us sit down on the edge of the dock. Lexie dangles her feet, and one of the enormous fish swims up, mistaking her toe for popcorn.

Lexie flaps her hands and laughs. And then it becomes a game where she lets fish after fish tickle her toes.

We feed the rest of the popcorn a handful at a time, our audience of fish faces staring up at us in rapt attention. Lexie reaches down every minute or two to touch a head.

"Is it weird being famous, Thomas?" I ask, without looking at him.

"A little," he admits.

"I can see how it would be."

"You know just because you achieve some success doing something you love to do, and people you don't know all of a sudden know who you are, you haven't actually changed inside your own head. I'm still the me who couldn't get a date my whole freshman year in college."

"I find that hard to believe," I say.

"True fact. You can ask Holden."

I give him a skeptical look.

"And the first time Holden and I played this little dive

club in Atlanta, we got booed off the stage. They actually threw baskets of pretzels at us. The hard kind."

"Did not," I say, trying not to laugh.

"Did, too," he says, grinning. "What's the difference between us then and us now? I couldn't tell you. We've got a little more polish, I guess. But I don't think we're that different."

"Maybe it's that social proof thing. People need to know other people think you're good before they can think you're good?"

"Kind of like the chicken or the egg. Which comes first?"

"I find it hard to believe anyone ever denied your talent."

"And I would say the same about you."

"We are so not in the same league, Thomas."

"Just because you don't see yourself that way doesn't mean the rest of the world won't."

"You don't have to say that."

"I know I don't. But I'm saying it because it's true. Play me a song tonight?"

I look at him then and smile a little. "Maybe."

♪

23

Thomas

Kiss So Good

It turns out to be one of those days I know I will never forget. A day I wish didn't have an ending, but might stretch on into infinity.

I don't think I can even explain what it feels like to be with Lila and Lexie. But it's like we've always been. Maybe it's because Lexie is a part of us both, the cord that ties us together. There's no awkwardness, just this comfort that feels like I've found a place where I belong.

We get back to the house around seven. Lila takes Lexie to her room to give her a bath, while I offer to make the only pasta dish I know how to make. Spaghetti with olive oil and Parmesan cheese.

Lila brings her back in a bit, smelling sweet in her pink pajamas, her wet hair in pigtails.

We eat outside on the deck, and my cooking appears to be a hit.

Lila cuts Lexie's noodles into bite-size pieces and puts a spoon in her hand, now and then helping her scoop some up. We talk about the fish we saw, and at the first mention of them, Lexie's eyes light up. She points at her toes and smiles.

"That's right," I say. "You almost lost a few today, didn't you?"

She giggles, and the sound of that fills my heart with overwhelming love.

As soon as she's finished eating, she starts to rub her eyes, her blinks heavy and slow.

"I think the sun wore you out," Lila says. "Why don't we get you to bed?"

"Want me to help?" I ask.

"That's okay," Lila says. "I'll tuck her in."

I kiss Lexie on the top of her head and tell her good-night.

I clean up and get the dishwasher started. I'm out on the deck, leaning on the rail and looking out at the night closing in on the water beyond the house when Lila comes back out.

"Hey," she says, walking over to the rail, but leaving space between us.

"Hey. She down for the count?"

"Pooped."

I look at her for a moment, taking in the contentment on her face, recognizing it as the same thing I'm feeling. "It was a good day," I say.

"A great day," she agrees. "Thank you, Thomas."

"You don't have to thank me. I loved it. Although, you do owe me a song."

The darkness has settled in around us. A boat or two whirs in the distance. A bird whose sound I don't recognize starts up a melody.

"Are you just doing this to be nice?" she asks.

"Actually, I'm not. I really want to hear you."

"I don't have my guitar."

"You don't need it."

She sighs and shakes her head. "Okay, but I can't face you."

I smile a little. "I'll turn the other way."

I get up and position my chair so that it's facing the lake. "Anytime you're ready, take off."

She clears her throat, and I hear her fidgeting. She starts off with a soft hum, and then dips into the first verse. The night goes silent around us. I close my eyes and focus on the sweet tone of her voice, the words so rich with emotion that my heart is instantly snared. And the chorus:

I want to live this life amazed

Hear the song

like it's never been played

I want to live this life amazed

See the world

Like it's my very last day

When she lets the last note fade from her lips, I slowly turn around and begin to clap. "That was incredible," I say. "You're incredible."

For a moment, just a moment, she lets me see how much the words mean to her. But then she shakes her head and says, "You really don't have to say that."

"No. I really don't. But I mean it."

I stand and push my chair back, walking over to stop in front of her. "It's okay to want it, Lila. To want something for yourself."

"There was a time when I did. When there was nothing I wanted more in the world. But that's not true anymore."

"Because of Lexie?"

"You can't have everything in this life, Thomas. I use to think that you could."

"In a town like Nashville, there are no guarantees. But

you've got talent, Lila. The real thing. And loving Lexie doesn't mean you can't be who you are. You're a singer. A writer. Repeat after me. I'm a singer. I'm a writer."

She play slaps me, laughing softly. "Stop. Why do you want to go getting a girl's hopes up when she's perfectly happy with things the way they are?"

"Are you?"

"What?"

"Perfectly happy?"

She turns away from me, leaning against the deck railing and staring out at the night-dark lake. "Don't," she says.

I step in to stand beside her, my arm against hers. "Don't what?"

"Make me want something I don't want anymore."

"If that's really true, I'll shut up right now. But you see, I don't think it is. I think you put your dreams away to do the right thing by Lexie. I can't tell you how grateful I am for the way you've taken care of her, even though I wish you would have let me help. We can't go back and redo any of that, but we can do things a little different from here."

"You and Macy have a lot in common."

"We both want good things for you, if that's what you mean."

"I don't mean to sound ungrateful. It's just that dreams come with price tags. Always."

I turn with my elbow on the deck rail, studying her profile as she stares out at the lake. She knows I'm watching her, but she won't look at me.

"Lila?"

"Hm?" she says, still without looking.

I put my hand to her cheek, slowly turn her toward me.

"Thomas," she starts, but I don't let her finish, settling my lips on hers before either one of us has a chance to rethink it.

My first thought?

I never forgot her. Never forgot this.

That little sound she makes when my mouth touches hers. The full, softness of her lips.

I half lift her to me, pressing her against the rail as our bodies remember the fit of each other.

She slides her hands up my chest, linking them at the back of my neck and letting me deepen the kiss. We lose ourselves to it, everything else falling away, my life in Nashville, her life here. It's just us. Finding each other again. And I wonder how we could have let this slip away the first time we found it.

"Baby, I could kiss you all night," I say, finding the side of her neck and breathing in her sweet scent.

She turns my face back to hers, and this time, she's

kissing me. With need. And hunger. And more than anything I've wanted in a long time, I want to fill that need. Satisfy that hunger.

"Lila," I say, lowering my head to kiss her neck and then her ear.

"We shouldn't be doing this," she says, her voice husky and uneven.

"Why not?" I ask, running my hands down her back to settle at her waist.

"Because. . .we. . .got ourselves in trouble the last time we messed around when we knew better."

"But you smell so good. . .and kiss so good."

Despite her protests, she interrupts me and finds my mouth again, and we both forget about all the reasons why this might not be such a good idea. She loops her arms around my neck, and it feels as if she could melt right into me.

The night is quiet around us, and I think we could be the only two people on earth.

I'm actually the one who pulls back first because I know if I don't, we're dropping over the edge, and we won't be coming back anytime soon.

"Lila. Dang, girl. You have any idea what you do to me?"

"If I do," she says, breathless, "I don't get it."

"What do you mean?" I ask, tipping my forehead against hers.

She pulls away then, turning against the deck railing to stare out at the dark lake. "Haven't you dated just about every single female singer in Nashville?"

"That would be a slight overestimation."

She shakes her head, and I see the smile on her face. "Slight."

"More than slight, then."

"Hmmm."

"Who I might have or have not dated has nothing to do with the fact that I'm clearly attracted to you."

She turns a little to face me then, her elbow on the rail. "Could we possibly live in more different worlds?"

"Again, I don't see what that has to do with—"

"It has everything to do with it," she says in a soft voice. "And even if that didn't concern me, the two of us starting this up again is nothing but a recipe for disaster."

"How do you figure that?" I ask, reaching out to run my finger along her cheek. She draws in an instant breath, as if I've scorched her skin. I have to admit I like seeing the effect I have on her.

"Lexie," she says. "If you're going to be a part of her life, Thomas, I want it to be because you really want to be in her life. Not because—"

"I'm trying to get you in bed?"

She doesn't answer my question, and all of a sudden, a wave of anger sweeps over me.

"Is that how you see me, Lila? You think I would play with her heart like that?"

I can see that she is regretting her choice of words, but I can also see that she really does think it's a possibility that I would. I move back a couple of steps in an attempt to sever the physical connection I still feel to her.

"I guess I don't really know," she says.

"Whoa," I say, running a hand through my hair and across the back of my neck. "You sure know how to put a fire out."

"Thomas, I'm sorry, I didn't mean—"

"It's okay," I say, letting out a deep breath. "You're probably right. We need to focus on Lexie and what's best for her. I'm sorry."

"You don't need to apologize, Thomas. I wanted to kiss you too."

"Well, that makes me feel a little better, anyway," I say, managing a half smile.

"We should go to bed," she says.

"We should," I say.

We study each other for a few, very long moments while a whole lot of things go unsaid.

Lila takes a step back, pointing over her shoulder. "I'm heading in then."

"I'm staying right here then."

She smiles and shakes her head. "You're a bad boy."

"What? No, this is me being a really good boy."

She turns and walks in the house, but I hear her laugh as she goes.

♪

24

Lila

Dreaming Awake

For the life of me, I cannot go to sleep.

And it's not for lack of trying.

I start to get up and take a shower as a diversion, but I can still smell a hint of Thomas's cologne on my skin, and I don't want to wash it off. I close my eyes instead and let myself be lulled into reliving his kiss.

It was every bit as good as I had remembered.

I'm not sure how that's even possible, because during the past six years, I had all but decided my memory had embellished his skill.

Apparently not.

The few guys I've been out with never once struck a chord of interest inside me. Of course the wall of resistance I put in place for them to attempt to climb over was pretty much unscalable, but I'm wondering now if the real reason was that I knew not one of them was ever going to compare to Thomas.

I'm not thrilled with my insight.

Because I'm nothing, if not realistic.

Me setting my sights on Thomas is the same as me deciding I'm not going to know a speck of happiness in life unless I win the lottery.

It's not like I don't know the odds of that happening.

And still. . .

The heart wants what the heart wants.

♪

THE NEXT THREE days are like something out of a dream.

You know how you sometimes have that feeling of having done something before? Deja vu? More than once, I feel like I've already experienced something we're doing. Like I've lived the moment before. And because that's not possible, I wonder if I dreamed it somewhere along the way. Maybe it's wish fulfillment.

Whatever the explanation, my dreams couldn't have done the real experience justice. It's like the rest of the world has fallen away, and we're in this perfect place where nothing matters except the fact that we're together.

I watch Lexie falling in love with Thomas. See her smile when he does some goofy thing that she finds adorable. Watch her slip her hand into his when we're sitting on the deck eating breakfast.

And part of me wants to stop her from falling for him. What if he decides he doesn't want to be a part of her life? Her heart will be shattered into a million pieces. At the same time I'm questioning it, I know I can't stop it. I have no choice but to let it happen.

And so I do.

We spend long, lazy days puttering around the lake on the pontoon boat. Getting out now and then in a secluded cove to float on the perfectly smooth water. Thomas never lets Lexie out of reach, and I'm amazed at how thoroughly I trust him with her safety.

Already, I know, that like me, he would lay down his life for her. Is there any more complete definition of love than that?

♪

25

Thomas

Can't Miss Another Thing

If I ever doubted my own self-control, I think I've pretty much affirmed its existence since our first night here at the lake when I kissed Lila out on the deck. And when Lila kissed me.

I'm not going to leave that part out, because it's true that we wanted each other. Still do if the invisible electric current I constantly feel between us is anything to go by.

But every time I look at Lexie, I think about what Lila said, and I realize she's right. This isn't just about the two of us. There's our daughter to consider. I guess I'm starting to see my attraction to Lila through the lens of what happens if I screw up. If we don't work. If one of us decides it's not what we thought it was.

I've missed the first six years of Lexie's life. If I know anything, it's that I don't want to miss another day of it.

And so, I put myself in the friend zone, not letting my gaze linger on Lila when it has the opportunity to do so. Making a constant effort to neutralize the desire I have a great deal of trouble keeping off my face.

One thing I'll say is this: it sure as hell isn't easy.

♪

26

Lila

What This is About

I invite Macy over for dinner on our fourth night at the lake house.

She knocks at the door a few minutes after six. I let her in, and she looks at me with a slightly dazed expression. "This place is incredible," she says.

"Temporary," I say. "Don't worry. I'm not letting myself get use to it."

"I could certainly get use to it," she says, glancing up at the high ceilings and wide, open, living room in front of us.

"Come on in. Thomas and Lexie are on the deck."

She follows me out, and I admit it feels a little awkward showing her this place. It's not mine, after all, and neither of us has ever known this kind of living before.

When I open the sliding glass door, Thomas picks up Lexie and walks her over to give Macy a hug.

"Hi, big girl," Macy says, kissing her cheek. "I've missed you."

Lexie hugs her back in her sweet, special way.

"Hey, Macy," Thomas says. "Glad you could come."

"Thanks for inviting me," she says. "Can I help with something?"

"Think we've got it under control out here. Lila, you want to show her around?"

"Sure," I say.

Macy links her arm through mine, and we go back inside, wandering through the kitchen and then each of the bedrooms, including the master one which Thomas insisted I take with its oversize Jacuzzi and view of the lake.

Macy falls onto the bed, arms and legs splayed wide. "Wow. This is incredible."

"Yes," I say. "An incredible vacation."

"You sure it's not more than that? Y'all look like you've been together forever."

I sit down on the bed beside her. "Thomas wants to be in Lexie's life. That's what this is about."

"Um-hm. How does that explain the way he looks at you?"

"What do you mean?"

"Like he wants to devour you."

"Does not."

"Does too."

"Anyway, it doesn't matter. We've agreed that Lexie needs to be our focus. And that anything between us would just put what's best for her at risk."

"How do you figure?"

I give her a sideways look. "Macy. Be real. What's the chance of anything between us actually lasting?"

"I don't have a crystal ball, that's for sure. But I'd say you have more of a shot at it than most of us. You do have that little girl in common, after all."

"So I should snag him with the do-the-right-thing hook?"

She play-slaps me. "That's not what I'm saying."

"It sort of is."

"You do have an advantage other girls don't have with him."

I give her a sideways look. "You know I don't think like that."

"Well, maybe you should."

I shake my head. "No."

"So what's next for you two?"

"He wants us to go back to Nashville with him." I expect Macy to leap off the bed in full cheerleader mode. But she doesn't.

I lean away and look at her. She's trying hard to smile, but the tears in her eyes give her away.

"And you're going, right?" she asks. "It's what you deserve, Lila. You can't let this ship sail by you. There's nothing here for you."

"You're here."

"And what can I do for you? You've got a gift, and you've got a daughter. Both of which you need to protect. You can't do that here."

"I've been doing it."

"And it's about to wear you out. Plus, I don't think they're going to hire you back at Smart-Send."

"That's a tragedy."

We both laugh a little, even though I'm fairly sure it could still be a tragedy.

"Dinner's ready," Thomas calls from the living room.

"Coming," I answer back. I stand up and say to Macy, "Let's go eat."

She reaches for my arm and turns me to face her. "When that truck of his pulls out of here headed back to Nashville, you and Lexie need to be in it."

I slide my hand into hers and pull her up from the bed. "Anybody ever call you bossy?"

"Once or twice," she says. "But I'm okay with it."

♪

LEXIE STARTS TO cough during dinner.

At first, I think she might have breathed in pollen or dust, but it continues to deepen, and by the time we're finished eating, she sounds really congested.

Thomas looks at me with concern in his eyes. "Should I run out and get something for her?"

"I have medicine, but it's all back at the trailer. I could borrow your truck and go get it."

"You shouldn't go over there by yourself this late," he says.

"Why don't you go with her?" Macy suggests. "I'll stay here with sweet pea."

"I'll be fine by myself," I start to protest.

"If you don't mind staying, Macy, that would be great," Thomas says.

"I don't mind a bit. We'll snuggle up in front of the TV, won't we, Lex?"

Lexie looks at her and yawns, then coughs.

"Why don't we get your jammies on first?" I say, getting up to lift her in my arms and carry her to her room where I change her clothes and brush her teeth.

Back in the living room, I set her down next to Macy and kiss her on the forehead. "We'll be back in just a bit," I say.

"We're all good," Macy says, tucking Lexie under the curve of her arm and starting to flip through the channels with the TV remote.

Thomas and I head outside to the truck. We drive the first few miles without saying much. An awkwardness has settled over us when we're alone now. As if we're both aware of what we want to happen, but can't acknowledge it or admit it.

♪

27

Lila

Need

It's kind of a relief when we get to the trailer. I get out and pull my keys from my purse, opening the front door. I hear Brownie's tail thumping against the barrel, and I know he wants me to walk over and say hello. But Rowdy's truck is parked in the driveway, so I don't.

Inside, I find the plastic container of medicine I keep in the kitchen cabinet, and pick out the things I think we'll need. Thermometer. Meds. Measuring spoon.

Thomas waits in the living room, standing in front of the window with his hands shoved in his pockets. I know he's looking at Brownie, thinking the same things I've been thinking from the first day I saw him tied to that awful barrel.

A door slams. Brownie whimpers, and then Rowdy's harsh voice shouts something I can't make out. I run to the window where Thomas is looking out.

"What is it?" I ask, worried for Brownie.

"Somebody needs to kick the crap out of that lowlife," Thomas says, without telling me what just happened.

I squint into the darkness, making out Rowdy carrying Brownie over to the truck and dropping him into the back like he's a sack of grain. He hooks a chain to his collar, and Brownie hunkers down out of sight.

"He never takes him anywhere," I say. "What is he doing?"

"Nothing good. I'm pretty sure of that," Thomas says.

I am suddenly overwhelmed with fear for Brownie. Tears well in my eyes. "What should we do?"

"If I go out there right now, he's not going to let me have him without calling the police."

I nod, knowing he's right. "We could follow him," I say.

Thomas considers this, then says, "I'm pretty sure it won't be the smartest thing we've ever done."

I'd like to disagree, but I have a feeling he's right.

We wait inside the trailer until Rowdy's taillights disappear around the first corner. Then we run out to the truck, and Thomas guns out of the driveway, lights off to keep us from being spotted.

By the time we get to the main road, Rowdy is nowhere in sight.

"Which way did he go?" I ask, panicky now.

"We're gonna have to guess. Left or right?"

Knowing Brownie's life might depend on it, I say a silent prayer for the answer before saying, "left."

Thomas swings the truck onto the road, and within a minute, we spot Rowdy's truck up ahead. Brownie is standing with his head over the side, his ears blowing back, and I could cry for the fact that he is probably excited to be going for a ride and thinks Rowdy is doing something nice for him for the first time in his life.

I'd like to think he could be right, but I know Rowdy. He doesn't have it in him.

We hang back far enough to keep Rowdy from noticing us. I have a sick feeling in my stomach because I'm remembering all the times he threatened to let Brownie "prove his manhood" by making him fight another dog.

"Where do you think he's going?" Thomas asks.

"I don't know," I say hesitantly, afraid if I voice my fears out loud, they'll come true. And then, "He use to brag about how he could take Brownie to a dogfight and make a whole lot of money. Where else would he be taking him this late at night?"

"Damn," Thomas says. "Hold on, though. Let's not do the deep dive yet. Maybe he's taking him somewhere to leave him because he doesn't want him anymore. People do that, don't they?"

"Loser people," I say.

"I'd put him in that category."

"I'd actually be relieved to know it was that. At least he would have a chance."

"We won't let him out of our sight," Thomas says.

I hear the concern in his voice, and something in my heart melts a little. There are a lot of things a guy can do to prove himself to a girl. Shower her with material evidence of his affection. Take her out to fancy places.

But those aren't the things that do it for me. Nothing slays me faster than a guy who can show compassion and kindness. Especially when it's for a dog who's spent his whole life on the end of a chain and whose breed alone has given him a reputation he's never done anything to deserve.

"Thank you," I say, looking at him long enough to let him glance over and see the tears in my eyes. "You're a pretty amazing guy, you know that?"

He can't hide his surprise. His eyes widen. "So that's the

secret then to winning your heart? Chasing around the countryside after a dog in need of saving?"

I smile. "Pretty much."

"That's how Holden won CeCe. I guess I shouldn't be too surprised."

"Are you going to explain that?"

"He helped her get her dog, Hank Junior, out of the pound one night after I let him get away. Really, no one else ever stood a chance after that."

"She sounds like an awesome girl."

"She is," Thomas says. "You remind me a lot of her. I think you two would really like each other."

"I can't imagine actually ever meeting her."

Thomas shrugs. "She's just a girl who likes dogs and music. Like you."

"I'm pretty sure that's where the comparison ends," I say.

"You might be surprised," he says. "Come with me to Nashville, and you can see for yourself."

"You're getting good at working that in," I say, trying not to smile.

He gives me a pointed look, his grin weakness-inducing. "I'm definitely getting better at it."

We drive for another fifteen minutes, mostly silent, as we wind through curvy country road after curvy country road. I'm thinking about Brownie again, and I just so do not have a good feeling about this.

"Do you think he would really make Brownie fight?" I ask, hearing the worry in my voice.

Thomas looks at me with a neutral expression, and I can tell he's trying not to let me see he's worried too.

Rowdy's signal light starts to blink, and up ahead we see him swing a left onto a gravel road. Once he's out of sight, Thomas makes the turn and flips off the headlights, pitching everything in front of us into darkness.

"Can you see?" I ask, panicking a little.

"Not much, but I don't want him to see us."

We roll slowly down the road, catching a glimpse every minute or so of the back of Rowdy's truck. It disappears over a knoll, and we slow down and wait a few moments before stopping at the top of it.

Below us, there's a small building surrounded by a couple of dozen cars. I lower my window and hear music blaring into the night with a big, heavy beat. Somewhere under the music's drone, I hear dogs barking.

"What is it?" I ask, my voice shaking out the question because I already know the answer.

"Probably what we were hoping it wasn't," he says.

"What are we going to do? We can't let him take Brownie in there."

"We'll leave the truck up here and walk down."

"And what do we do when we get there?"

"I haven't figured that part out yet."

"Are you sure this is safe?"

"No," he says. "But I think Brownie's going to need the cavalry. And we're the only one he's got."

He parks the truck on the side of the road, and we both jump out. We run the quarter mile or so to the building, stopping far enough away that we're still in the shadows if anyone looks our way.

The music is really loud with a deep bass, but I hear snarling inside the building, some cheering and clapping, followed by some booing.

"I think I'm going to be sick," I say.

"Don't think about it," Thomas says. "We're just here to get Brownie."

I spot Rowdy's empty truck parked close to the building. "Do you think he's already gone inside?"

"It looks like it. You stay here for a minute and let me get a closer look."

Fear clamps tight on my chest, for Thomas, for Brownie. "I don't think you should go inside."

"The tailgate's down on the truck, so he's already taken Brownie in. I'll be back, okay?"

But just as he starts toward the building, Rowdy opens one of the doors and drags Brownie out with a heavy link chain around his neck. Brownie is whimpering.

"You loser piece of shit," Rowdy roars at him. "Is that all you've got? Lay down on your belly and give up? I'll show you give up!"

He aims a kick at the center of Brownie's belly, knocking him to his side. Brownie cries out, trying to get up and run, just as Rowdy grabs the chain and jerks him back.

I scream at the top of my lungs. "Stop! Stop it!"

Thomas is tearing full out across the parking lot. He launches himself at Rowdy, taking him down in one crushing tackle.

Rowdy hollers like he's been stuck with a bayonet. Brownie tries to get up but falls over on his side and lies still.

I stumble to him, dropping to my knees while tears gush up and out of me, spilling down my face. "Brownie, it's me, Lila! Brownieeee!"

I smooth my hand across his side, trying to find any wounds he might have. There's one under his belly, a rip of flesh. When I pull my hand back, my palm is full of blood.

"Thomas, he's hurt!" I yell, crying full out now.

But he's still rolling Rowdy across the gravel parking lot. I don't know if Rowdy has an ounce of muscle on him, but he's got enough fat to make it hard for Thomas to get out from under him.

I run over to them, grabbing Rowdy's oily T-shirt and yanking him backwards. The shirt rips, but he topples and flops onto his side.

Fury erupts inside me then, and I start kicking him, hard and anywhere I can land my foot. "You evil bastard!" I scream at him. "How could you do that to him?"

Thomas is up now and hauling me off Rowdy. "Lila, stop. Enough!"

I scream in frustration because I want to kick him until he's lying as still on this ground as Brownie. Behind my fury, tears pour from me, and I am suddenly sobbing so hard I can't breathe. "If he dies," I gasp, "there is going to be a special place in hell for you."

"As soon as I. . .get up from here. . .and get my gun out of the truck," he shouts, "I'm going to shoot the worthless mutt like I should've done a long time ago."

Whatever reprieve Thomas was prepared to grant him goes up in so much smoke, because he jumps him again, punching him in the face and then straddling him to hold him on the ground.

He leans in close to Rowdy's sweaty face, threatening him through clenched teeth. "We're going to leave here in thirty seconds with your dog, and if you so much as come within a mile of him or Lila ever again, I will personally kick your balls so high up your throat, they'll double as your tonsils. Are we clear?"

The heat of hatred coming out of Rowdy's eyes could melt asphalt, but he nods a small nod.

Thomas gets off him then, brushing his hands across his jeans as if he can't stand the feel of Rowdy on them. He backs away from him, then takes my hand, and we run back to Brownie.

He hasn't moved since I left him.

"I think he's in shock," I say, between sobs.

Thomas drops to his knees and lifts Brownie into his arms. "Come on, boy. Let's go get you some help."

We start back up the hill, trying to run, but Brownie is heavy and Thomas is trying not to jostle him too much. We're halfway back to the truck when I hear a sound I almost recognize but not quite. When I realize what it is, I stop suddenly, knowing what's coming, even as I'm helpless to stop it.

"Thomas!" I cry out, just as the shot rings through the night.

I expect it to hit me, wait for the pain to ring out inside my body. Almost simultaneously, I see Brownie's body jolt once, and his scream tears open the darkness around us.

Thomas falls to his knees, and I am instantly terrified that he also has been hit. He tries to protect Brownie from the impact, landing on his left shoulder so that he takes the brunt of the fall.

And now I'm screaming, terror for them both cutting off my ability to breathe. I drop to my knees, see the gaping hole in Brownie's shoulder. Blood is pouring from it.

"Thomas! Are you okay?"

He groans and starts to get to his feet. "Yeah. You look after him. I'll be right back."

"Wait! You can't–"

He's already charging at Rowdy, who looks as if he's just been blinded by headlights. Even from here, I see the intent on Rowdy's face. He raises the gun, points it at Thomas. He fires, and I am instantly frozen with fear that it has hit him.

But the bullet misses, and Thomas keeps running. When he's almost on him, Rowdy drops the gun and turns, taking off in the opposite direction. Thomas jumps him in seconds, yanking him down. He pounds him with his fists until awareness slumps out of Rowdy, and he's lying face down in the dirt.

Thomas stumbles to the back of the truck and grabs the chain Rowdy had used on Brownie. He wraps Rowdy's wrists together with it and then links it to his ankles so that he's not going anywhere without help.

And then he's running back to us, half limping, his face stiff with pain.

He drops to the ground beside us, looking at Brownie's wound with the same fear in his eyes that I'm feeling.

"We've got to get him to a vet. Fast," he says. "Where's the closest place?"

"It's about ten miles from here," I say. "Will that be fast enough?"

"I don't know," he says, shaking his head. "We have to try."

He squats next to Brownie, sliding his arms under him and scooping him up like a baby. Brownie is motionless, and I am so scared for him that I can't force myself to move.

But Thomas is already carrying him to the truck. I run around him and open the back door. He slides him onto the seat and looks at me with this look that tells me how much he cares about what happens to Brownie.

"We can't let him die," I say, tears again streaming down my face.

"Get in," he says. "We don't have a minute to waste."

I slide in from his side, but instead of moving all the way to the other door, I stop in the middle. I want to be near Thomas. I need to feel his strength next to me. I wonder how I could ever have thought I didn't need him.

Because I do.

As he turns the truck around, gunning it down the

narrow road, I slip my arm through his, and lay my head on his shoulder.

I need him.

♪

Next: Nashville – Part Six

Nashville - Book Six - Sweet Tea and Me

THE NASHVILLE SERIES
BOOK SIX

sweet tea
and
me

RITA® AWARD WINNING AUTHOR

INGLATH
COOPER

Books by Inglath Cooper

Swerve

The Heart That Breaks

My Italian Lover

Fences – Book Three – Smith Mountain Lake Series

Dragonfly Summer – Book Two – Smith Mountain
Lake Series

Blue Wide Sky – Book One – Smith Mountain Lake
Series

That Month in Tuscany

And Then You Loved Me

Down a Country Road

Good Guys Love Dogs

Truths and Roses

Nashville – Part Ten – Not Without You

Nashville – Book Nine – You, Me and a Palm Tree

Nashville – Book Eight – R U Serious

Nashville – Book Seven – Commit

Nashville – Book Six – Sweet Tea and Me
Nashville – Book Five – Amazed
Nashville – Book Four – Pleasure in the Rain
Nashville – Book Three – What We Feel
Nashville – Book Two – Hammer and a Song
Nashville – Book One – Ready to Reach
On Angel's Wings
A Gift of Grace
RITA® Award Winner John Riley's Girl
A Woman With Secrets
Unfinished Business
A Woman Like Annie
The Lost Daughter of Pigeon Hollow
A Year and a Day

Get in Touch

Email: inglathcooper@gmail.com
Facebook – Inglath Cooper Books
Instagram – inglath.cooper.books
Pinterest – Inglath Cooper Books
Twitter – InglathCooper
Join Inglath Cooper's Mailing List and get a FREE ebook! Good Guys Love Dogs!

Made in the USA
Middletown, DE
23 March 2019